MADAM

X

MADAM X

L.J. DIVA

★ Royal Star Publishing ★

Chances is an imprint of Royal Star Publishing
www.royalstarpublishing.com.au

First edition paperback published in 2025
All Rights Reserved, Copyright ©L.J. Diva 2025

Trade Paperback ISBN: 978-1-922307-96-5
Large Print Paperback ISBN: 978-1-922307-97-2
Dust Jacket Hardcover ISBN: 978-1-922307-98-9
E-book ISBN: 978-1-922307-95-8
A catalogue record for this book is available from the National
Library of Australia.

Cover design: Royal Star Publishing and ©Designed with Grace
Cover photos: Cityscape: 4LUCK/shutterstock.com
Typesetting in Minion Pro by Royal Star Publishing

DEDICATION

This series is dedicated to the crime fighting Reagan family, especially Sean. Sometimes, *Blood* is not thicker and definitely not *Blue*, and the truly wrong will always pay for their sins.

Chapter 1

"Who's been a bad boy?"

Crack!

The sound of the whip against the flabby white ass of the man rang out in the sex room of the infamous Madam X.

"Oh, I have, Madam, I have," the man quavered. It wasn't just his voice that quivered, but every nerve ending in his rotund body.

"Is it good?"

Crack!

"Oh, yes." His voice barely a whisper as sweat dripped down his face and back. His hands were tied to the wall above him, but his body was sagging as his knees did. They were weak, like the rest of him. He was an overweight, popular politician in the city of New York who got off on having his ass spanked with a whip, who got a hard dick from being tied up, and who had to come every night during the week.

Madam caressed her black riding crop while staring at the blubbering mess of a man. "Have you been a bad boy?"

"Yes, Madam, yesss ah!" He arched towards the wall as the pain seared through his flabby left ass cheek. "More, more."

Madam slashed the whip across his lily-white ass five times on each cheek, then stood back and sighed. "We are done. Get dressed." She untied his hands and watched him slump to the floor. "You can leave via the back way as usual."

"Thank you, Madam," he whispered, and hauled himself up from the floor.

Bernard Dietrich was a fifty-two year old Slovakian born, American made man who had tastes and fetishes that were hard to accommodate. Prostitution was illegal in New York, but strangely, BDSM was a grey area. He could go to a street whore, but sex wasn't what he got off on. Having his ass spanked and being tied up was. He quickly gathered his clothes and dressed, knowing she was still in the room, watching.

"Thank you, Madam." He zipped up his pants. "Same time tomorrow night?"

"Of course, Bernard. You're one of my best regulars. Always arrive on time, and always pay on time. I'll escort you out." Madam watched the man slide on his blazer, opened the sex room door, and turned to her left, opening the door to the back garden and undercover walkway. "Is your driver ready?"

Bernard checked his watch. "He should be in the garage."

"Good night then, Bernard." She glanced over the grey haired man and inwardly sighed. He'd been a client for thirty years and she doubted it would stop. But, like all the rest, she was making a killing out of him. The only nights he had off was Saturday and Sunday. Five nights a week he visited her, and she loved the money it brought in.

She glanced down the walkway and saw that the light above the stairwell up to the garage was on, which meant there was a car waiting for its passenger. "Looks like he's ready. Stay safe, Bernard. I'll see you tomorrow night."

"Yes, Madam," he muttered, and furtively looking around, dashed along the walkway to the stairs and up to his waiting car where he climbed into the back seat and lay down.

The driver backed out, and Madam's driver, Rocco, closed up the garage doors.

She waited for him to hurry into the basement before triple locking the heavy wooden door. "That's the last one for the night. You can go home now, Rocco."

"Ma'am." He gave her the once over, observing black patent leather corset and knickers with matching stilettoes, black lace stockings and garter belt. Her hair was rolled up into a twist, and she wore a black and silver sequin fancy dress mask with black feathers around the top of the eyes.

"Don't look at me like that, Rocco." She pulled off the mask and sighed. "It's what keeps you in wages."

"Yeah, but for how long?" He followed her out of the basement. She donned a dressing gown as they went upstairs to the front door. "This shit's illegal, you know. When are we gunna be busted?"

"I don't know, Rocco." She opened the door and let him out. "It could be any day, which is why I'm always prepared. Drive safe." She locked the vestibule and front doors behind him and sighed. This life was getting to be too much. Six nights a week she and her girls serviced the powerful bigwigs of New York; the girls with sex, she with whips and chains. Each man who came through her doors had a fetish of some kind, and she wrote every single one down. She was Josephine Pompadour, Madam X to the rich and famous of New York City. The Big Apple, the city that never sleeps. And neither did most of her clients.

Josephine stood for a moment in the silence of the hallway until the grandfather clock in the parlour chimed for two in the morning.

That was her cut off limit for those who needed to sneak in and out in the dead of night. Two a.m. The last had gone, and so was her energy.

She slid out of her shoes and picked them up, noticing Hilda, her pink dressing gown covered housekeeper, peeking over the first floor balcony. "It's time for bed, Hilda. See you in the morning."

"Is there anything you need before bed, ma'am?"

Josephine slowly climbed the stairs in her stockinged feet. "No, thank you. Everything's locked up downstairs and Rocco's left. You, Fanny, and Myrtle should be in bed."

"We were, but I heard you. The kitchen's locked up tight unless you want something." Hilda Gerhard had been with Josephine for over fifty years. She had started under Josephine's mother when *she* was Madam X, not long before Josephine took over. She had remained faithful and loyal and would do so until her dying day, even though she didn't agree with what went on in the house. It had been a solid income for the last five decades, and the job had been her one go-to after her husband died. So when Josephine asked her to move in, she jumped at the chance. Her children didn't like it, of course, but they had no say in what their mother did.

"No, thank you, Hilda. You go back to bed because that's where I'm heading." Josephine reached the first floor and slid her arm through her housekeeper's. "You go. I'll await breakfast at eight sharp, as always."

"Yes, ma'am." Hilda escorted her mistress up to the top floor and hurried back down to the small room she had for herself as the housekeeper, while Fanny and Myrtle shared a room.

Josephine's sanctuary was on the top floor of the brownstone; the servants had the two bedrooms on the fourth. It was a five level, red brick building that was lavishly decorated in fine antiques, crystal, and china. Rich, luxurious fabrics were used for the curtains and bedding, and velvet covered all of the couches and chairs. The furniture was rich mahogany; many antiques passed down from Josephine's mother and grandmother.

Josephine locked her door and slumped against it, a sigh leaving her in a rush.

At seventy-two, maybe it was time to give this all up. Give up the late nights, the ass spanking, the rule breaking politicians and judges and lawyers.

"I think I'm too old for this shit," she muttered, and walked over to her Victorian three door three drawer mahogany wardrobe. She dropped the shoes on the floor in front of it, slid off her dressing gown and threw it on the bed, popped open the buttons on her corset and unzipped it, breathing another sigh of relief as her rib cage expanded. "I really am too old for this shit." Josephine quickly pulled off her attire and threw it into the wardrobe before sliding back into her gown. She padded into the small black and white decorative tiled bathroom she had to herself. Normally, old brownstones wouldn't have en suites for bedrooms, but when she'd taken over from her mother she'd transformed the top floor into a sanctuary for herself. A spacious bedroom with its own bathroom.

She turned on the taps above the claw foot cast iron white bath tub, and brushed out her hair, braided it, then pinned it up so it didn't get wet. When the bath was full, she slid into the steamy, lavender-scented water.

She scrubbed herself clean and then relaxed for fifteen minutes. When the time was up, she stepped out and drained the water, dried herself with a thick Egyptian cotton pale blue towel, and slathered her body in rich cocoa butter moisturiser. She cleaned and washed her face with one of the top skincare products currently available in New York, and unpinned her hair. After giving herself the once over in the mirror, she padded across the thick velvety carpeting of her bedroom, slid into a white wrist and ankle length nightie with a high frilled neck, and settled into her soft-as-a-cloud four poster bed with the velvet canopy and a luxurious European comforter.

She sighed and contemplated quitting the business. Then she contemplated doing without all of the money. Then she contemplated what would happen if she was arrested and her lips slid into a sly little smile. If that was ever going to happen, then thousands of careers would be destroyed.

She fell asleep with the smile on her face.

*****

He held one nostril closed, snorted a line of coke through a rolled up twenty up the other, and threw his head back, sniffing and wiping his nose. "Good shit."

"Gonna share that with us?" Benito asked, watching his friend snort another line up the other nostril.

Carmelo wiped his nose and shook his head. "Not this shit. It's too good for the likes of you. Besides…" He unrolled the twenty and licked it clean of drugs. "You can get your own. I had to scrounge for this from my source."

Carmelo wiped up the remnants from the glass and licked his finger. No grain was going to be wasted, and certainly not shared with his gang. He ran a hand through his thick black curls and leaned back in his chair, putting his boot-clad foot onto the coffee table in front of him and pushing off, balancing on two chair legs.

At twenty-nine, he'd been the leader for five years, fighting the former boss to death for the role. Benecio Jacopo had been the leader for ten years, but had taken a bad batch of drugs and tried to kill off his entire gang. Only Carmelo stood up to him and landed a knife in his chest. He'd aimed for his heart, and scored. Benecio was dead, and Carmelo became the leader of the Little Italy East Side Gang.

Benito grumbled and glanced around at the gang members present. Enzio Vittorio, Fabio Donato, and Pasquale Claudio. The others were patrolling the grounds, or off doing other things. "We're having a meeting tonight. Not everyone's here. Some said they weren't coming."

"They can go then." Carmelo took a swig of his beer. "I see the hangers-on are here instead." He motioned at the wannabe gang members. "Think you can handle it?"

The five boys, ranging in age from eighteen to twenty-five, nodded.

Benito glanced over his shoulder. "Hey, kids. What'ch'ya names again?"

One by one they called out.

"Dino."

"Vincenzo."

"Nico."

"Salvatore."

"Angelo."

Carmelo slammed his chair to the floor, rocked to his feet and stalked over to the five boys, giving them the mandatory once over. "You're too skinny. You're too fat. You're too hairy. You're too ugly. You're too…" He stared at the young man. "Who're you again?"

"Angelo." The boy of eighteen, with dark curls framing his cherubic face, and dark lashes fanning above his blue eyes, shyly smiled up at him. "And you're Carmelo Fortunato, the leader of the gang. I've heard about you my entire life. I wanted to be you, at one stage. You're famous."

Carmelo frowned. "Yeah…" he muttered, staring down at the boy who distinctly reminded him of himself at that age. Just seven years ago. How could he have wanted to be him his entire life? "You're too good looking. You'd be a distraction to the gang. There's no point you being here. Leave." He waved him off and walked back to his chair. "We're not initiating at this time, but what I want to know—" He broke off and stared at his gang members one by one before adding, "is why the hell are none of the others here? Everyone comes to meetings regardless of what's going on."

"No idea," Enzio muttered, sucking on his cigarette. "But who cares? If they don't want to be here, kick them out. Get new members."

Carmelo considered his comment. "I may have to. If you're not going to turn up to the gang meetings, then you shouldn't be in the gang. Period."

"Can we join, then?" Salvatore called out. He was the one Carmelo considered fat, and he was determined to diet and exercise from that day on, if it meant he got into the Little Italy East Side Gang.

"No!" Carmelo glanced at them and saw Angelo looking hopeful. Nope, there was no way he was going to let a kid that looked just like him into his gang. He'd worked too hard to be leader, resorting to overdosing Benecio to make him psychotic and to give a reason for killing him. No one was going to take over. He was the leader. That was that.

*****

"So who are you here to see?"

"Charisse. You?"

"Tallulah."

"I haven't tried her yet. What's she like?"

"Amazing. Sucks dick like nobody's business. Yours?"

"Takes it up the ass like a champion. Have you tried any of the others yet?"

"Seriously, gentlemen." Josephine swept into the parlour of the brownstone in her Victorian era rich burgundy velvet off-the-shoulder dress with multiple ruffles down the back trailing behind her. Her long grey hair was swept up into a chignon with a ruby clip on the side, and ruby earrings hung from her delicate lobes. A matching necklace completed the set. "Is that how you talk about my girls while you're waiting?" She glanced from man to man, and shook her head. "Little wonder how you speak of me when I'm not around." She sent a scathing glare to the two perpetrators. "Benedict, Prentiss. I expected better from a police officer and a lawyer."

"Madam." Benedict gave a sharp nod. "You are correct. And my, don't you look elegant tonight? That tone of red suits you." He quickly sent glances to each of the men waiting in the parlour.

Prentiss Adair was a lieutenant in the NYPD, Everett Lloyd was the current DA, Bartholomew Winthrop the top judge in the city, Howard Herschel a bigwig movie producer, and Harlan Conway owned the hottest men's magazine in the sex and porn business.

They nodded in agreement, murmuring words of praise for her outfit.

"Your flattery and praise will get you nowhere, so I warn you against insulting my girls." She glared at each of them. "They may service your fetishes and sexual needs, but they are not to be treated with disrespect, understood?"

More nods and murmurings.

And she didn't believe any of them.

Josephine's glare homed in on Bartholomew. "Well, Bartie, you're up. Harmony is waiting for you in the red room. You know the way, don't you? Or do I need to put in an elevator for you and your tired old legs?"

Guttural laughter mocked him as he managed to stand.

"My legs aren't that bad, Madam." He shuffled over to her and nodded. "Red room's on the first floor, right?"

"That's right. The one you have every time you're here," Josephine said. "Upstairs, last on the right." Tapping her red lace fan against her left hand, she watched him grasp the banister and slowly make his way up. Finally, she turned back to the men in the room. "Your ladies are also waiting for you in your rooms. Treat them with respect, or you will not be seeing them again. You know the rules."

"Yes, Madam," they murmured and quickly made their way upstairs or down to the basement to three more bedrooms along with the sex room.

The first floor had been sectioned off into four bedrooms five decades earlier when Josephine's mother had the work done to accommodate more men at any one time. The basement had three bedrooms set up, along with the sex room, and the top two floors were kept as the private suite for the owner. Now they housed Josephine and her staff.

Josephine wandered down the hallway to the kitchen and sat heavily on a chair at the table. "They're with their girls. Be aware they may start ringing for more champagne and hors d'oeuvres at some point."

"We have it all ready, ma'am." Hilda nodded to Fanny and Myrtle. The three of them made sure the household ran smoothly and food and drink was brought in, along with anything else the men might require. "What about you? Do you need anything?"

"No. I'm going to retire to the library while we wait. The sex room is not needed tonight, and no one else is coming." Josephine paused a moment. "On second thoughts, I'll have a cup of tea, and some of those delicious cookies you make, thank you." She rose and slowly walked out of the room.

"Of course, ma'am." Hilda nodded and started preparing it.

Josephine walked into the library; a lavish room between the kitchen and the parlour, filled with floor-to-ceiling shelves groaning under the pressure of wondrous books from all over the world. She turned on the light by the window and sat in her high-backed Rococo Revival chair, put up her feet on the matching foot stool, and sighed. It was going to be a relatively quiet night and she wanted to finish the book she had started a few days ago. She picked it up from the table beside her, found her place, and began to read.

*****

"Oh, Bartie, fuck me, fuck me," Harmony cried as she bounced away on his dick. "Fuck me with your big fat cock, Bartie. Fuck me."

Her fast, breathy gasps turned him on, and he clawed at her curvy hips as she bounced. His heart pounded in his chest in time with the pounding on his cock. "Oh, God, I'm coming. I'm coming." His heart exploded in his chest as he exploded in her. "Fuck me!"

"Oh, Bartie," Harmony panted and fell onto his chest. "You and your cock do it every time. You know how to make me come so hard and fast." Her fingers traced the lines on his chest, and miss-stepped the grey hair so they didn't tangle in the sweaty mass. "You know how to fuck me, Bartie. I'm still throbbing. Champagne?"

She bounced up to sit on his chest, her knees under his armpits, and grabbed the bottle of champagne from the ice bucket on the bedside table. Her blonde curls mixed with his, but she ground into them, regardless of the sweat she didn't want her fingers in. "You need to fuck me again, Bartie." She took long gulp of champagne, letting it drip down her chest, swallowed and gasped, rubbing the drips into her voluptuous breasts. "Want some Bartie boy? Or do you want to drink it from my body?" She tipped some between her breasts and watched it run down her abdomen to her crotch. It tingled in her privates and she ground into him. "Want some, Bartie?" Holding the bottle to his lips, she tipped it up. "Drink away."

He gulped and pushed it away. "That's enough. I need to sit up."

She leaned up on her knees while he pulled himself up and then settled back on him. "What now, Bartie?"

His hands roughly moved up and down her legs and into the thick thatch between them. He played with her clit and made her squeal, made her head fall back, and the bottle drop from her fallen hand. "I want to fuck you every which way, Harmony. I want to touch and lick and bite and scratch every part of you, especially this part."

His hands lifted her up and planted her on his mouth. He sucked and licked and inserted his tongue into her, making her cry out.

"Oh, Bartie, fuck me with your tongue." Harmony grabbed him and clung on, a useless rag doll in his arms. Most clients didn't do anything for her, but for some reason, Bartholomew Winthrop did. Maybe it was his big dick, or his big tongue and mouth. "Fuck…Bartie." She fell backwards onto the bed, legs bent back under her, her pussy near his mouth. He pushed up to a sitting position, arms around her waist, holding her to him, slurping on her pussy as if he was French kissing a French bulldog.

She was vaguely aware of wrapping her legs around his neck, and even less aware of him crossing his legs over her neck to push her breasts towards him for optimal groping. He continued until she convulsed and came in his mouth. He slurped like a starving dog until it stopped. Then he uncrossed his legs, rolled her over, and climbed on for his finale. He came and grunted to a halt.

"Oh, Harmony. That was the grand finale of my life," he panted in her ear. "I want you every time I come here." He laid his head on hers and waited for his heart to stop pounding. "I want to do it with you every time, Harmony. I want to fuck you and have you fuck me." He lifted his head to look at her, wiped away her hair from her face, and froze. "Harmony?"

He checked her breathing and found none. He shook her. "Harmony. Harmony. Oh, no, no, no, don't you dare die. Harmony." He managed to get to his knees on the thick bedding of the four poster and shook her.

"Harmony. Wake up. Harmony. Oh, God." He shook her more. "Harmony, no, no, no. Harmony."

When he couldn't wake her, he panicked. "Oh, my God. What do I do, what do I do? I'm a judge for fuck's sake. I just killed a whore. What do I do?" Bartie glanced around the red room, so red it made his vision blur to the same shade. He shook his head and it cleared enough for him to see the phone on the bedside table. He grabbed it and called downstairs.

"Is there anything you need?" Hilda asked. It was part of her job to cater food and drink, and knew exactly which room was calling. It was an in-house system Josephine's mother had set up.

"I need Madam X," Bartie whispered. "Something's wrong."

Hilda breathed in sharply. "I'll send her up," was all she said, and hurried to the library where she shook Josephine awake. "Ma'am, ma'am, you need to get up to the red room. Something's wrong."

Josephine stared at her and checked the mantel clock for the time. Eleven thirty-five. "What the hell is going on?"

"Mr Bartholomew just rang and said he needs you. Something's wrong."

"Damn it!" Josephine hurried from the room and up to the first floor where she entered the room without knocking. She hit the light switch and the room flooded into a bath of yellow white. "What's wrong?"

Bartie was hovering at the wall beside the bed, holding a blanket in front of him. He pointed to Harmony.

Josephine closed the door and rushed over to her girl. "Harmony. Harmony." She shook her and rolled her over.

"Harmony. Wake up. Harmony, come on, wake up now." She felt for a pulse, but there was none. "What the hell! Harmony." She slapped her face and shook her. "Harmony." When there was no response, she put her ear to Harmony's chest and listened. There was no heartbeat. The only sound in the room was Bartie's whimpering. "Do shut up, Bartie, and get dressed. What the hell have you done?"

Shocked and disgusted, Josephine leant back and stared at Harmony. "What the hell do I do? I only know a certain amount of first aid. I suppose an officer or lawyer would—" The light bulb went off over her head and she rushed from the room and into the blue room next door. "Get dressed. We need your help."

"Hey," Prentiss complained as Charisse was pulled off his cock. "What the hell, Madam?"

"We need you in the red room, now. We need CPR. Get your pants on." She grabbed his arm and pulled him off the bed. "Now. The red room. I'll get Benedict." She hurried from the room, and headed next door to the green room. Each room was lavishly decorated in a different colour to make it easier for the men to follow directions. Men could be such simpletons at times.

"Benedict, I need you in the red room, now." Josephine pulled him off the bed, and off Tallulah. "Sorry T, I need Benedict's legal expertise. Get dressed; at least put on your pants. Now."

She hurried back to the red room to see Prentiss hovering over Harmony and Bartholomew still cowering in the corner, fully dressed. "How is she?"

"Dead," Prentiss said. "How long?"

"No idea." Josephine looked at her watch. "Maybe ten,

fifteen minutes."

"Yeah, then she's dead." Prentiss glared at the judge. "You killed her?"

"No," he quavered, hands grasped to his chin. "I… she…no…"

Benedict rushed into the room. "What did you get me out of bed for…oh…" He stared down at the naked body. "Damn, Bartie."

"It wasn't me," Bartie cried. "I didn't."

"You did!" Josephine screamed, spinning around to hurl her fists at him. "You killed my girl, you fucking bastard. And now what? What am I meant to do about it? Call the cops? You fucking killed my girl."

"It was an accident." Bartie cowered to the ground, covering his face with his arms while the others tried pulling her away. "I don't know what happened."

"Bullshit," she spat. "In the entire time this establishment has been here, there has never been a death until now. And you. And what am I meant to do with her body?" She slumped onto the bed and stared at Harmony. "What am I meant to do with you?"

Prentiss turned to the judge. "What happened? The truth."

Bartie shook. "I was sucking her pussy. She wrapped her legs around my neck and I crossed mine over hers. She came, she was alive, and then I rolled her over and fucked her from behind. When it was over she wasn't breathing, so I rang downstairs. I don't know what happened."

"More than likely asphyxiation by way of a stupid sex position," Prentiss said. "What do we do?" He glared point blank at Benedict. "What do we do with her body?"

"I'll call the morgue." Josephine wiped the tears from her cheeks. "I'll call now."

"No." Benedict stopped her. "This can't get out. No one can know she came from here. They'll realise what this is and what she was doing. We need to be careful or all our reputations will be on the line." He grasped Josephine's shoulder hard and she glanced up sharply. "And who do you think will get the blame? Not us."

She shoved his hand away and stood up. "Are you threatening me, Benedict Manning? Because if you are, I will warn you to think very carefully about continuing to do so."

"I'm simply telling you what will happen if you call the morgue and this gets out," he said. "Don't do anything stupid."

She pointed at Bartie. "*He* already did."

Chapter 2

"I'm sorry," Bartie sobbed. "I'm so sorry."

Josephine, dressed in her Madam X attire, whipped the judge in a fury. The lashes screamed red raw marks across his white flabby skin. Her frenzy was from his murder of Harmony two weeks ago. She had been on the lookout in the papers and on TV for anything that might suggest a girl had been found and that she was a hooker with her establishment, but there had been nothing. No news about it at all. All thanks to the cover up by Prentiss and Benedict, no doubt.

They hadn't been in attendance for the last two weeks, but Bartie, oh no, he had been coming every night for a whipping; paying his penance for Harmony's murder.

"Am I bleeding?" he gasped, sagging to his knees and crumpling against the wall. He was tied to a wall rack so he couldn't move, but the bonds weren't that tight and the ropes allowed him to slide down.

"Yes," she murmured, her panting quiet in the room. "Not much, but some. My staff will clean it up before you go home." She threw the whip onto a nearby bench and slumped against it. "Why, Bartie? Why? You know what this means, right?"

"Oh, Madam. I'm so sorry," he whimpered. "I must be punished and this is the only way."

"Not the only way. You could give yourself up to the police, resign as a judge, and quietly do your time." She breathed in slowly, deeply, into her gut, staring at the wall in front of her, tears welling in her eyes. "How could you?" she whispered. "How could you?"

Harmony had been one of her top girls; the one most excited about this life. All of them were paid well, per john, and Harmony was investing in herself. She was attending university to earn a degree as a veterinarian, and was trying to save enough to set up her own practice. Only then would she get out of the business she was in.

Josephine had wanted to contact her family, but didn't know who, or where, they were, and Harmony hadn't spoken of them. No one had been on the news looking for her.

But, she thought, *it's only a matter of time before someone does.*

"I don't want you here anymore, Bartie," she said softly. "I can't risk it."

"Oh, Madam," he cried. "Please don't say that. You're the only one I come to. The only one I *can* come to. Where else would I go? *Who* else would I go to?"

Josephine glared at the whimpering figure on the floor; an old, soft man in his seventies who thought being a judge gave him a free pass. It didn't. And one day, he would pay. It was just a matter of when. "I can't have you here anymore, Bartholomew. I just can't."

"What if I make it up to you?" He struggled against

his bonds to sit up properly. "I can donate to your favourite charity; deal with any fines or legal matters you may have. I can do something for Harmony. She was my favourite."

"She was your only," Josephine muttered through a clenched jaw. "And now she's gone and what the hell am I to do?" She spun around, and backhanded the whip across the face.

He cried out and hung his head in shame. "That hurt."

"Good," she screamed. "It was meant to. And now it will mark you and your shame until you repent." She moved around him and resumed whipping his back. "Repent. Repent. Repent," she screamed over and over, whipping him until his blood flowed freely.

*****

"So what do you think happened?"

"With what?"

"Bartie and that girl?"

"Who knows? We shouldn't be talking about it."

Harlan Conway glanced around the prestigious gentlemen's club on Fifth Avenue where he and Howard Herschel were lounging, smoking their Cuban cigars, and drinking scotch, neat.

Howard furtively glanced around at the other men in the room to see if they had overheard. "We shouldn't be talking about it. Not here, not anywhere." His gaze landed on Harlan. "Are you going to print anything in your magazine?" As a movie producer, he was always on the lookout for something to produce; an idea, or story… He could get some screenwriter to write it up, find a director, or do it himself, and then produce it into a multi-million dollar property. He was also on the lookout for new talent, and often found them in the pages of Harlan's magazine. He had a penchant for young women, eighteen to twenty-five, and liked having his ass spanked with a ping pong paddle. He also liked having the ping pong ball shoved between his ass cheeks and then having it belted by the bat. One time, it had been lodged in and he required a doctor to get it out. Fortunately, there had been one at Madam X's when it had happened, and he'd removed it. It certainly hadn't stopped Howard from doing it again.

At sixty-five, you needed to get high from all the shit you could try because you just couldn't get a hard dick from any of it anymore.

Harlan, seventy years into his life with short grey hair parted on the side, a red Chinese silk smoking jacket wrapped around him, and a cigar permanently in his right hand, waved him off. "Howard, you need to stop worrying. The boys took care of it. She's gone. None of us know where. Just lie low for a while and we'll forget about it in a month or so."

Howard shook his head. "I don't know if I'm going back there. I don't know if I can. We were there that night, Harlan. Doesn't that worry you, or freak you out? Madam told us not to come back for a while, but going without is making me weak."

"You were always weak and insipid," Harlan snarled. "You need to grow up. Be a real man for once in your pathetic life." He shoved his cigar into his mouth and inhaled long and hard. He hadn't been in the business of men's magazines for fifty years without learning something. Learning to keep your mouth shut when you needed to, exploiting what you couldn't stop talking about…that's why he'd been the number one magazine owner the entire time. He exploited what he could. But the death of a hooker in a brothel by a judge… That was something he couldn't talk about, or exploit, because that could lead to all sorts of questions being asked about how he knew.

"Thanks for the insult," Howard spat. "I don't need it from you." He glanced at the man trudging through the door. "Good God, is that Bartie?"

They watched the judge shamefacedly glance around the room, notice them, and waddle over, ignoring everyone who called out to him.

"Gentlemen." He sat in the wingback chair next to Herschel and winced at the pain in his back. "Have you been back yet?"

"No, we thought it best not to. You?" Howard asked.

"Every night for the last three weeks, to repent my sins." Bartie glanced over his shoulder to see who was watching. Or listening. "I'm paying for them."

"How's that, exactly?" Harlan looked over Bartie's shoulder to see curious expressions. "Looks as if people are wondering why you didn't return their courtesies, or sit with them."

"I've taken time off," Bartie whispered. "I thought I should."

"When was the last time you did that?" Howard watched the waiter put a scotch on the coffee table in front of Bartie and walk away. "You're entitled to a holiday."

"Years." Bartie downed the scotch in one go and

waved for another. "Felt I should."

Harlan eyed the old man. "It's probably also time to go."

"How so?" Bartie asked and didn't let the waiter put down his second scotch. He grabbed it from his hands and downed it as well. "Another, please." The waiter was surprised, but hurried away. "As I said. How so?"

"Retire, get away from it all." Harlan took a drag of his cigar. "Go to the middle of nowhere and live out the rest of your life."

"I wish," Bartie mumbled and nodded at the waiter when he put his drink down. "I wish I could. But I must repent, and deal with the consequences of my actions."

"And what are those?" Howard asked.

Bartie glanced over his shoulder to see who was close enough to hear before leaning forward and whispering, "MX is seeing to it. Whipping me into penance. She banned me from the red, but holds me to account in the basement."

Harlan perfectly understood what he meant. "The wicked MX. And how is your pathetic weak flesh?"

Bartie's face grew red. "Marked."

"As red as your face and that mark across it, I imagine." Harlan chuckled. "Serves you right. We haven't been back since that night. You ruined it for the rest of us, you pathetic pile of shit. You really need to grow up and take responsibility, Bartie."

Bartie sipped his scotch. "I know, that's what I'm doing."

"Getting your ass whipped is not taking responsibly," Harlan replied. "Be a man. Deal with it and leave."

"As if *you* would," Bartie countered. "You wouldn't just turn and leave without another word. I'm a judge—"

"Retire!" Harlan snapped. "You're old, so retire and go away. You have nothing except your law degree and even that's nothing but a worthless piece of paper now. I have a magazine empire. I can't walk away."

"Oh, of course not," Bartie snarled. "Big Harlan Conway couldn't just walk away from his magazine empire. If we're found out, Harlan, we're all going down. Don't expect me to save you."

Harlan's deep, loud baritone laugh rang out in the parlour of the club and all eyes turned to him. "That's a good one. I have my own lawyers and can buy my own judges. I don't need you, Bartholomew Winthrop. You're nothing but a weak insipid man who can't do anything right. Time for you to retire, *Bartie.*"

Bartie glanced to Howard. "And what do you have to say?"

Howard looked from him to Harlan. "Nothing. I am not getting involved in this conversation."

"Weak. All of you." Harlan grinned, showing off his new dentures. "Time to move on and move out. Both of you."

*****

Prentiss walked into the *Ballroom* on the Lower East Side and took a place at the bar. On a Friday night, it was the local haunt for cops and lawyers who worked on the upper end of the island of New York and wanted to hide from their colleagues and work acquaintances, so he knew he might see one or two who had been dealing with not going to Madam X's for the last four weeks. It reeked of cigarette smoke and spewed up alcohol, but that added to the ambience of the place along with the pitiful music wafting through the overhead speakers, and the neon lights above the bar.

He ordered a whiskey and glanced around, spying a few fellow officers by the jukebox waiting for the pool table to be free. He turned back to the waiter and downed his drink. "Another." He banged the glass on the bar and waited for it to be refilled.

Taking a sip, Prentiss spun around on his stool and saw Benedict cowering in the corner of a booth on the other side of the room. He sauntered over and slid in across from him. "Benedict."

Startled, Benedict pushed himself hard into the corner. "Prentiss. I didn't see you. When did you come in?"

"A few minutes ago."

"And why are you sitting here?" Benedict glanced around, making sure no one was watching.

Curious, Prentiss asked, "What are you scared of, Benedict?"

Benedict's gaze finally landed on him. "Everything," he whispered.

Prentiss laughed. "You are kidding? What, you got a felon who's after you or something?"

Benedict leaned in and whispered, "No. MX and Bartie."

Prentiss's breath caught in his throat and he paused while his heart pounded for a few seconds before he forced it to calm down. "What Bartie did was stupid and we had to fix it. No more favours for that asshole." He finished his whiskey and played with the glass. "No one can find out what we did. You hear me, Benedict?"

"What *you* did, you mean," Benedict replied. "I just

made suggestions. You actually did the deed and no one knows what you did because you said you'll keep it to yourself."

"The less known, the better," Prentiss replied. "It's like that joke. What happens when a judge, a lawyer, and a cop walk into a brothel?"

"That's no joke," Benedict muttered under his breath. "Bartie can lose his job. So can we. And MX banned us for a month."

"She didn't *ban* us." Prentiss scowled. "We all suggested that we take a hike for a month and lie low until it blew over. No one's found out anything, so far."

"And I see no body's been found." Benedict stopped nursing his bourbon and finished it off. "No body. Where was it?"

"The less you know the better." Prentiss waved at the bartender for another whiskey. "But no one will find it."

"What about the family?"

"What about them?"

"They must be wondering where she is."

Prentiss shook his head. "Nothing's happened so far, and I'm keeping my ear to the ground for any noise about it." He nodded at the waiter who delivered his drink. "You want anything?" he asked Benedict.

"No, thank you." Benedict shook his head at the waiter and watched him walk away. "I need to know what's going to happen. It could ruin my reputation."

"Guess we all should've thought of that when we started going to MX then, shouldn't we." Prentiss took a sip of his new drink. "Really, Benedict, we're all in it up to our necks. Just like every bigwig in the city is up to their neck in something. Dodgy building practices, breaking the law, dodging reports, getting criminals off."

A deep, heavy sigh came out of Benedict. "I've tried to keep myself clean, and I've succeeded so far, but Bartie is going to bring this down for us."

"That's if MX allows him back." Prentiss studied his companion's face. He'd aged a good ten or twenty years in the last month. "You going back?"

Benedict shook his head and shrugged lightly. "I don't know."

Prentiss looked around the bar and saw some of the officers looking his way. He nodded and took a swig of whiskey. "I'm going to play pool with my fellow officers. Keep your nose clean, Benedict." He went to move, but Benedict's hand snaked across the table and grabbed his arm.

"What did you do with the body?"

Prentiss removed his hand and leaned across the table as he stood. "Not going to tell you." He left Benedict frowning and worried for his life.

*****

"Oh, yeah, baby, suck it." Carmelo grabbed the girl's hair and held her head to his crotch. She was sucking hard on his cock and he jerked forwards as he came. "God, fuck." He moved back from the wall he'd been leaning against and pulled her to her feet. "You know how to suck good. Wanna do some more?"

"Depends." Kaylin wiped her mouth with the back of her hand. "What are you up for?"

Carmelo looked around the black room in Madam X's basement. It had black velvet walls, lush black carpeting, a four poster bed with black bedding and canopy, and black shaded lamps were dotted around the room giving off an eerie glow. He liked it and had done so the first time he used it, and asked to keep using it for his trysts with Madam X's whores. It was black, like his hair. Like his mood. Heading up one of New York's biggest street gangs was hard work, and he didn't want a street whore, so he came to the best brothel in all of The Big Apple. Madam X. Quiet, secretive, clean. So were the girls. "Get on the bed while I suck you."

Kaylin, a young, twenty-something blonde, dutifully crawled onto the bed and lay sideways against the pile of pillows.

"On your back," he commanded, and watched her naked body slide down until she was flat. He launched himself onto her and grabbed both breasts, devouring them with his hands and mouth. She squealed, but he kept up the pressure, making his way down her body to the delectable pussy covered in white blonde hair. His tongue went to work as his hands held her down and she grabbed his hair to cling on.

He launched up and slapped her across the face. "Don't touch my fucking hair," he yelled as she cowered on the bed, covering her wounded face. "You fucking bitch. You don't touch the fucking hair." He shoved his finger into her face. "You got that?"

She gave a scared nod of her head and whimpered, crying out as he dragged her body down the bed and onto her stomach.

"I'm gonna teach you not to do that again, bitch." He shoved himself into her and fucked her hard, making her cry out in pain. When done, he sucked the place he'd just been in and dug his fingers into her ass cheeks. His tongue then latched onto her anus. It was a fetish he'd had since his teen years, and he sucked even harder.

She clawed at him, trying to get him off. "Help," she screamed at the top of her lungs. "Help me."

"No one's coming to help you, bitch," he growled and shoved his penis into her anus. He roughed her up, not even hearing anyone enter the room above her cries for help until the click sounded in his ear.

"Get the fuck off her."

He looked up in surprise to see Josephine holding a gun to his head.

"*I said, get the fuck off her.*" Her eyes bored into his, fury and anger emanating from them. "And don't ever come here again, Carmelo Fortunato. You are now banned. Do you understand me?"

Carmelo glanced from her to her driver who held a shotgun aimed right at him. "Ah, yeah." He quickly pulled out and knelt on the bed. Both guns moved closer. His hands went up. "Hey yah, yeah, okay. I get it."

"Kaylin, go up to my room and wait for me. I'll take care of the trash," Josephine said, and waited for her to grab her robe and run out of the room. "If it's one thing I don't tolerate, it's the bad behaviour exhibited towards my girls. *No one*, and I *mean* no one, abuses them, or assaults them. Do you understand me, you cunt?"

Carmelo, wary of two guns pointed at him, slowly nodded. "Of course, Madam X. It was just some rough play. She loved it. Isn't that what they're here for?"

Josephine stared him down. "Get dressed, get out, and never come back. I don't want you here again. Got that?"

"Sure, sure." Carmelo slowly backed off the bed. "I'll just get dressed and leave. The back way, as usual." He eyed off the two guns and grabbed his pants from the back of a chair. "I'll just get dressed."

"Make it quick. I want you gone," she said coldly and waited for him to dress. When he was done they escorted him to the back door and Rocco followed him to the garage to let him out.

"You can make your own way home, since your driver's not here." Rocco pushed the gun closer to him. "Get out and don't come back."

Carmelo eyed the gun and grabbed the door handle. "Tell Madam she's going to pay for this."

"Tell yourself that you're going to pay for hurting her girl. Get out." Rocco waited for Carmelo to leave then locked the door up tight. He sighed. What a douche.

*****

Josephine waited for Rocco to enter the basement and locked up. "Wait for a while, in case he comes back. I'm going upstairs. There's no one else down here." She hurried upstairs to the top floor and entered her room. "Kaylin, I'm so sorry."

Kaylin was sitting on the bed, wrapped in her robe. "Why didn't you come?"

"I did, sweet girl. When I saw him slap you, I acted. I grabbed my gun, got Rocco, and came as fast as I could."

She sat on the bed beside her and smoothed back her hair. "I'm so sorry. I did warn you all when you started that some of them might get rough. You all said you were up for it. And luckily, you're the first who's been assaulted."

Luckily?" Kaylin snarked. "Oh, I'm so comforted by that, Madam. So, so comforted. I hurt, all over, especially my ass."

"How's your face?" Josephine looked at the red mark across her cheek. "That will heal, and it will take some time for the other thing to heal. We can get in the doctor for a look if you like, make sure everything's intact. And then you can have the next month off."

"Oh, lucky me. Getting a month off. You'll be lucky if I come back." She stormed around the room. "I *did not* sign up for rough anal sex and being slapped around. That is *not* something I'm going to tolerate as a part of this job. I'm glad it's only happened once, and yes, you did do something about it," Kaylin made hand movements in sync with her words, "but I'm not going to put myself in danger again. I'll take that month and then decide if this is something I want to keep doing. You got that?" She panted heavily and gripped the post of the bed, clinging to it as the tears came. "I can't do that again."

Josephine moved to her side and rubbed her back. "There, there. We can organise things to be different. You can refuse anal, if it's not your thing. Pick something else to be an expert at. All of our clients like some thing or another; they all have fetishes. You can pick which one to service."

"Ha! That's a joke," Kaylin mocked and let out a deep sigh. "I just don't know."

"I'll call in Dr Cullen. He'll come and fix you right up and then we'll drive you home. You'll be right as rain in no time." She hurried over to her desk and found his number, calling him even though it was eleven-thirty at night.

"Dr Cullen."

"Josephine Pompadour. I need your help."

There was a pause so long she didn't know if he was still there. "Hello."

A sigh. "I'm on my way."

When she hung up, she dialled down to the kitchen. "Hilda, make a nice pot of tea for me and Kaylin in my room. The doctor's on his way, and she needs her clothes. Can you gather those things, please?"

"Of course, ma'am. I'll send Fanny up with them when she finds them, and bring the tea shortly. Would you like something to eat?"

"Some of those cucumber sandwich triangles, please. I am rather famished."

"Some soup, too?"

"Yes, just a cup, for both of us."

"Ma'am."

Josephine placed the phone into its cradle. "Dr Cullen is on his way, Fanny will bring up your clothes, and Hilda will bring up something to eat. Rest until they come."

"How am I supposed to do that?" Kaylin argued. "My ass hurts like hell."

"Lie on your side." Josephine rushed over to the bed and flung back the comforter. "Lie on your side. Rest until the doctor gets here."

"What will happen to him?" Kaylin asked, awkwardly

lying on her side and tucking several pillows under her head.

"Who?" Josephine pulled the comforter over her and sat beside on the edge of the bed.

"That john. I don't even know his name."

"I've banned him, and told him he's no longer welcome here." Josephine glanced around her room and sighed. "In all of my years doing this, I've never had a girl assaulted." She remembered back a month ago to Harmony. "Killed, yes, but not assaulted."

"Killed?" Kaylin perked up. "Who was killed? Did I know her?"

"No," Josephine said sharply as a knock sounded on the door. "Come in."

Fanny, the maid, came in with a bag of clothes. "Your bag, Miss Kaylin."

"Thank you, Fanny. Set it on the trunk at the end of the bed. Is the doctor on his way?"

The doorbell rang out, and a second later it was answered and closed.

"Guess he is. The food should be on its way too." Josephine stood as Fanny left and Hilda came in with a tray of food.

"Here you go, ma'am. Doc's right behind me. A pot of tea, some soup, and sandwiches." She set the tray on Josephine's desk. "Anything else, ma'am? Do you want me to pour?"

"No, thank you, Hilda. You go, and close the door after the doctor. Ah…" She saw him enter the room. "Here he is now. Thank you, Hilda." She nodded to the doctor and waited for Hilda to leave the room. "Kaylin needs to be examined."

"What happened?" Russell put his bag on the end of the bed and pulled out a pair of white surgical gloves to put on.

"A john got brutal," Kaylin told him, and flung the covers back. "He slapped my face and was rough up my ass."

Russell glanced at Josephine. "And what did you do?"

"Shoved a gun in his face and banned him from my establishment," she replied, holding up the teapot. "Tea?"

His sigh was full of exasperation. "Thank you. Okay, let's get you examined. Roll over." He thoroughly checked Kaylin over, and while she was red and sore, nothing was torn. "You'll be sore for a few days, but everything's intact." He ripped off the gloves and shoved them into his bag. Digging around, he found a small tube of cream. "Here, put this on once a day and try not to pass faeces for a couple of days. If you have to, go, but be careful how you clean yourself and then wipe more cream on afterwards."

"With what?" Kaylin took the tube and stood up. "My finger?"

"Smear a small line on a piece of toilet paper and dab it to your anus." Russell shut his bag and accepted a cup of tea from Josephine. "Your face is fine, no broken bones. You'll heal."

"Thanks, Doc. I'm gonna get dressed. Do I put some on now?"

"Not if you plan on a shower when you get home. Do it after."

"Okay." Kaylin grabbed her bag and hurried into the en suite.

"How is she?" Josephine sipped her tea and studied the doctor.

"Fine. How's the perp?"

"Probably angry that I threatened him. But I'll blow his balls off if he comes back. They know the rules when they start. Otherwise they aren't accepted. Sandwich?"

"No, thank you." He glanced at the tray and salivated. "Damn, I am hungry. And it's late."

"Just one?" Josephine asked, setting it onto a small plate.

"Fine." He rolled his eyes and set his cup down on the desk. "I shouldn't be here. Especially this time of the night."

"Why? Had you gone to bed?" Josephine nibbled on a quarter cut of sandwich. "Whatever will your wife think?"

"That I'm having an affair," he managed around his food. "I shouldn't be here. I shouldn't be your doctor."

"Then who would be?" She took a sip of tea. "You've been our doctor for thirty years. I pay you well."

"You do, and it's paid for my house and car and put my kids through school, thanks very much, but it's taking a toll. Not just on me, but you and the girls."

Josephine's brows furrowed. "How is you being our doctor taking its toll on me and the girls?"

Kaylin barged out of the bathroom. "I'm ready. I'm gonna head out. Will Rocco take me home?" She grabbed a sandwich off the plate and shoved the whole thing into her mouth.

"He will." Josephine picked up her phone and called her driver. "Take Kaylin home please, and then head home yourself." She picked up another quarter of sandwich. "Tea or soup?"

"No, just sandwiches." Kaylin grabbed a second. "I'll

go and wait downstairs. Thanks, Doc. Madam." She left the room and hurried downstairs.

Josephine looked at Russell. "She seems fine. Magic cream?"

"Something like that." He paused, looking at her with concern. "You all right, Jo?"

Her smile was brief. "Yes, Russell. I'm fine. *Now.* Not last month." The smile fell away and her brows dipped. "But then again…"

Russell heard the grandfather clock in the parlour ring out. "Damn, midnight. Gotta get home." He gulped down the rest of his tea, burning his throat in the process. He followed it up with another cucumber triangle sandwich to cool it.

"Why? Do you become a werewolf at midnight?" Josephine joked.

"Something like that," Russell quipped and slid into his jacket. "I'll see myself out." He rushed from the room and Josephine rang downstairs for Fanny to let him out and lock up.

Sighing, she finished off her tea, another sandwich, and her cup of soup. It was a delicious meal for such a cold, late night, not too heavy for her shrinking stomach.

Once Hilda had retrieved the tray, she showered, and settled into bed for a good night's sleep.

Chapter 3

"Cyrus."

"Allen."

"Donald."

"Allen."

"Ambassador."

"Allen."

The men stood around the banquet table in the function room at *The Carlyle Hotel*, attending a gala honouring Cyrus Stratton's fifty years as a politician. In a lavishly decorated room, with a table laden with the finest food one could import, the hotel was hosting the gala being held by the Republican party for its longest serving member.

Cyrus Stratton, happily married to the very French Veronique, his third wife, or so he'd tell you, had three sons in their forties by his first wife, and two daughters in their thirties by his second.

At seventy-one, he was fit as a fiddle, ate like a horse, worked out daily, and used Viagra when Veronique needed servicing. Or when *he* needed servicing. His silver grey hair was cut into a short and simple fashion, with a wave flowing to the right from his side part. His chic Parisian suits were the most expensive his wife could buy, and their old Victorian mansion on Fifth Avenue competed with their mansion in the Hamptons, and their mansion in Beverly Hills.

Allen Gerard, the mayor of New York, sipped his champagne while regarding Cyrus with a critical eye. "You look well. Your health regime must be working."

Cyrus chuckled. "Or so my wife thinks. I like to slip a hamburger or two into my meal plan."

Allen, having been in politics for forty years himself, nodded politely. He knew of Cyrus's penchant for hookers and whores. He saw him on occasion at Madam X's brownstone. "You like to slip into a hooker or two as well. Does she know about those?"

Startled, Cyrus choked on his champagne. "Don't you dare!" he furiously muttered under his breath and leaned in closer. "If you value your own career, you'll never mention such things again."

Allen smirked, and gazed around the ballroom to see some of the country's most prominent political figures, including the two that were silently standing with them now.

Donald Reinhold was a world renowned director of Jewish movies, and the ambassador was Dirk Ellison from Denmark.

"I doubt your wife will find out. Hell, I doubt any of our wives will find out. Besides," Allen said, and took a sip of his champagne, "as long as Veronique keeps looking the way she does, there'll be no problem with her getting your cock up."

"And *your* wife?" Cyrus arched a white brow. "Does she know about *your* penchant?"

"Of course not. But it's not as if *you're* going to tell her." Allen gave him a scathing glare.

He was interrupted by Bernard who took to the microphone on the small stage at the side of the room.

Bernard held his glass up and turned in their direction. "Ladies and gentlemen. We are here tonight to celebrate the great Cyrus Stratton and his fifty years in the Republican party." He stopped a moment for the wild applause. "Cyrus, come up and say something."

"Oh." Cyrus shyly waved him away. "I couldn't…"

The crowd urged him to go onstage, and he finally gave in.

"Okay." He walked over to stand next to Bernard who stepped aside. "Oh…" he said into the microphone and winced at the feedback. "Sorry about that." Gazing over the crowd, he saw that a good five hundred people were there to celebrate his career. He recognised many he knew personally, and some he didn't. "Thank you, thank you. I must say…" He smoothed his blazer and sent out a thousand watt smile. "I certainly wasn't expecting such a turn out. My time in politics has been long, and at seventy-one I have no idea how much longer I'll be doing it. I had thought of retiring at seventy-five, so that gives me four more years." Light laughter went around the crowd. "A part of me can't wait to retire. A part of me wishes I could work on until the day I die. Who knows, I certainly don't, but in the meantime, thank you all for coming here tonight to help me celebrate such a milestone in my life." His gaze landed on his wife and children. "Thank you to my wife Veronique for keeping me young enough to continue doing this, and thank you to my kids for supporting me even when I wasn't around, but I hope I can be a father to you now. Thank you so much for coming. Enjoy the food; enjoy the night."

He waved and stepped off the stage. He'd seen the filthy scowls from his children; five ungrateful retches who were only around for his money, prestige, and status. They didn't actually care about him or his career, or Veronique for that matter. He hurried into the arms of his wife and kissed her on both cheeks. "Ronnie, I'm so glad for your support."

"It's Veronique," she growled in his ear and he stiffened, then she smiled and planted another kiss on his cheek. "Darling, let me escort you around the party. It is for you, after all."

"More like to show you off," Karen, Cyrus's eldest daughter, muttered under her breath. She wore a simple Donna Karan black sleeveless sheath and matching flats, and plain gold jewellery. She stood with her arms crossed and a scowl on her face.

Cyrus heard her and glared at his boringly blonde plain jane daughter. "Can it, Karen." He left Veronique's grasp and moved over to his children, seeing four more scowls. "You didn't have to come tonight, children. You could have said no and I expected you to."

"Ronnie demanded we come," Heather, the youngest daughter replied. A replica of Karen, she wore a similar style of clothing. It was a style their mother had worn all their lives.

Veronique glowered at them. "I didn't demand. I just

made it clear this was a big deal for your father and you should be here." Her gaze travelled up and down the two women. "Still dressed by your mother, I see."

Their scowls deepened, but Cyrus laughed. "Leave them, my pet. If they want to be miserable all evening, let them. Let's go and mingle."

Allen watched the exchange from his vantage point beside the buffet table. "Seems Cyrus's children hate Ronnie's guts."

"Probably hate Cyrus's guts too." Donald knocked back his champagne and signalled to the waiter for another. "I could make a movie out of their drama."

"Why don't you?" Allen asked, putting his glass on the waiter's tray and picking up a fresh refill. "It would be quite interesting."

"It would. But, like the rest of us, it would out us all." Donald glanced around at the celebrities mingling with the politicians. "We can't risk that."

"Out us all for what?" Dirk asked. "I'm not normally here. Have I missed something? Like all of this gorgeous food. Anyone else hungry?"

All three eyed off the banquet table and made a beeline for it. As they filled up their plates, the conversation continued.

"Out us for the seedy underbelly that is New York," Donald said quietly. "We all get up to naughty things sometimes. Everyone in this room has."

Dirk glanced over his right shoulder at the crowd, and then his left. "Everyone?"

"Everyone." Donald confirmed.

"Even the waiters?"

"Well, I don't know about them," Donald said, exasperated.

"I'm talking about the celebrities and politicians."

"Including this guy here?" Dirk used his elbow to point out Allen.

"Even this guy here." Donald nodded.

"And what would the seedy underbelly be?" Dirk went on.

Donald looked him square in the eye. "Have you heard about Madam X?"

*****

Josephine locked the basement door behind the last john and sighed in relief. She rested her forehead against the wood and breathed evenly. The charade of this life was wearing on her. But, if she was to be honest, it had really worn on her since Harmony had been killed.

She'd had a lot of thoughts in the last two and a half months; thoughts about her life, her mother's and grandmother's lives. Whether she even needed to continue in it. Being a madam was a life she had not asked for; it was a life she had grown up in. And, unfortunately or otherwise, it was one she had taken over after the death of her mother, who had taken over after the death of *her* mother.

If being a madam ran in the blood, they were proof.

If it was a lifestyle choice…she'd disagree wholeheartedly.

She was considering retiring in three years at the ripe old age of seventy-five. But something had been nagging her. Nagging at her inner most core.

It was the thought that she would not see seventy-five. That was why she needed to make sure her will, money, paperwork, and ledgers were taken care of.

Breathing in, she pulled back from the door and wandered upstairs, seeing the girls coming down, dressed and ready to leave. "By the back door, girls. Hilda has food and drink in the kitchen if you're hungry. Take some home with you." She watched each as they passed her.

Portia. A curvy Italian with a mane of wild jet black curls, on her head *and* between her legs.

Shiloh. A slim, tall, blonde with Icelandic features was a dab hand at slapping any man into submission.

Giselle. German, brunette, and bawdy. She could make the men laugh while they sucked on her size 20 double D breasts.

Heaven. A sweet New Yorker with red hair and freckles to whom the men loved to reveal all of their secrets.

Josephine's smile was wistful as she followed them into the kitchen. It had been many a year since she'd come down those stairs after being in one of the rooms. And she preferred it that way.

"Girls, I made you some food to take with you." Hilda handed out the small plastic containers that held sandwiches and fruit and followed them up with colas. "Take a bottle of drink with you. Unless you want juice."

"How about wine, and lots of it?" Portia asked. "After the night I've had, I need it."

"Were they out of hand?" Josephine asked, standing inside the door. "Just tell me and I'll ban them for life."

"No." Portia shook her head. "I think I'm just done dealing with dickheads."

The girls laughed, and Josephine cracked a smile. "I know what you mean."

Portia flung her hair over her shoulder. "I'm done, you know. Having to listen to their sob stories about their wife not loving them, and being unable to get it up except when they're with me. That it's me they love, and me they want, and me that gets them hard. It's boring."

"Agreed," Shiloh said, shoving half a sandwich into her mouth. "I'm sick of hearing about my Icelandic features and how they'd love to see me in a Viking costume. Yuck!"

"We do have costumes if you need them," Josephine informed them. "Some of you have used them."

"I know, Madam." Shiloh threw her hand up in frustration. "I'm just sick of old dirty men. I don't even date because of this job."

Josephine perked up. "Do you want to leave? We can afford to have a few girls leave the business. There are plenty of you on rotation."

Shiloh stared coolly at her boss. "Yeah? I'll think about it. 'Cause really, I'm only doing this job for the money."

"Same here," Heaven agreed. "I'm over the men, too."

"Then have a serious think about it, and decide what you're going to do. Hell, I'm not even sure I'll last in this business much longer. I'm feeling my age and it's not getting any younger." She opened the back door for them. "Night, girls. Let me know what you decide."

"Night." They filed out one by one, down the back terrace stairs and through the back gate that Rocco held open. A taxi was waiting to take them wherever they wanted to go.

"Did I hear right?" Hilda asked. "Are you thinking of shutting up shop?"

Josephine locked the back door and let out another

deep sigh. "Just a thought that's been playing around in my head. In this business, we need to be careful, and prepared, for the law to be on our tail."

"Even though they visit here to get some tail?" Fanny asked as she tidied the kitchen.

Josephine smirked. "Yes, Fanny, even though that. Prostitution is illegal in New York, as is being a madam. I could be in a lot of trouble if they decide to turn tail and haul mine into jail. What would happen then? You'd be out of your jobs. So would the girls. They might be arrested for what they do. You could be too. And I probably wouldn't be let out. They'd keep me in as long as they could because they'd be scared I'd reveal all." She wearily seated herself at the kitchen table. "Let's have a nice soothing cup of tea to end the night. Everything's locked up, Rocco's gone home. It's just us left and it's late."

*****

The whip cracked against the taught ripe ass of Parker Grant. A hot twenty-five-year-old former child star actor, he'd been in the business for twenty of those years. He'd seen a thing or two in Hollywood and had moved to The Big Apple two years ago. With a penchant for ass whipping, he'd fallen into the right actor circles to find out where the best madam in town was, and thanks to his new circle of friends, had also redeveloped his penchant for drugs.

At fifteen, he'd been admitted to rehab for a year, and come out the other side with a new lease on life, becoming a bigger teen heartthrob than he had been going in. His life in New York was wild and eccentric and suited him to a T, along with his bisexual nature.

He screamed as the pain tore through his flesh. "God fucking damn it!"

"You wanted an ass whipping." Josephine set down her whip to pull on a thick workman's glove. The rough texture was perfect for gripping the genitalia of males and she had a large stockpile of them. "Now…Parker… because you've been such a bad boy, you're going to be punished and you have no say whatsoever."

"I'm already being punished," he muttered. Restrained against the wall frame, his hands and feet were tied to the wooden posts. While he could buck and writhe, he couldn't move more than that. "Give it to me, bitch. I'm ready."

Josephine's left brow arched. Dressed in her Madam X outfit, she picked up the whip and slammed it against his back. "Don't call me bitch," she snarled. "And just for that, you *will* be punished." The whip flew across his back, leaving scorching red marks on his skin. When she was done, she gripped his penis with her gloved hand, and roughed him up until he cried out and ejaculated, then attacked him with the whip again until he was sobbing for her to stop. "I'm done. And so are you if you ever call me bitch again. *I am Madam X, and you never call me anything other than that*," she snarled. "You will show respect to me, my staff, and my girls when you are in this establishment. Do you understand me?" She cracked the whip across his neck. "Do you understand me?"

"Yes, yes, Madam, yes." Parker's body shook with his

sobs. He'd never felt pain of this magnitude, certainly not when high as a kite, and not even in rehab. But the life he'd forged for himself in New York… He pulled himself together. "I'm sorry. I didn't know I couldn't role play. I thought that's what this was."

"No. It's pure BDSM." Josephine discarded the glove into the bin and set the whip on the wall rack. "You live out your fetishes and fantasies in this room, but you sure as hell never call me anything other than Madam because you are the submissive. Do you understand?"

"Yes, Madam," Parker sobbed. Josephine untied his left hand and it fell to his side as she untied the right. "Yes, Madam." It came out small and soft as he crumpled to the floor.

Regardless of his age, he was still very much a child and she looked down on him with pity. "Hollywood did a number on you, Parker. Don't let New York take you, too. Get a better crowd to hang out with, better management and friends. And maybe then, you will survive it. If you don't…you won't make it to thirty." She reached down and untied his feet. "Get dressed and leave. This is all you were here for. Rocco will be waiting in the garage."

"Yes, Madam," Parker mumbled and dazedly watched her leave the room. He fumbled into his clothing and out to the basement where she directed him outside, and he made his way to the garage where his driver was waiting. His obsession with having pain inflicted was wearing on his body. He would be marked for weeks, so it was just as well he didn't work for another couple of weeks and could take the time to heal.

He pulled a small zip bag of coke from his back pocket, licked his finger, and dunked it in before sucking it off. A quick hit was what he needed to calm the pain. It was not as though he was a junkie who snorted, injected, or swallowed. He just took quick hits throughout the day.

So much for rehab.

He watched the bright lights of the Upper East Side go by as his driver headed for his apartment in Brooklyn. The lights of New York dazzled him. They were different from the lights of Hollywood. Not fake or full of shit. Not calling to you to get involved in things you shouldn't. He liked the lights of The Big Apple, the city that never slept. Although he could. Some nights he took downers. Other nights he sat on the rooftop and stared across the river at the city, seeing the Brooklyn Bridge off to his left, and the Manhattan Bridge directly to his right. He had a bird's eyes view of the city he now called home. And it was one he liked very much.

*****

Josephine made her way up to the parlour to find some of the johns lounging around. "Gentlemen, are you not being serviced? Have you done your time? If so, why are you still here?"

"Madam." Donald nodded at her and silently admired the deep emerald green Victorian era gown she wore. "I'm waiting on my favourite girl. She's currently busy with Harlan."

Josephine looked at the grandfather clock. Ten p.m.

"His time is over. She'll be ready for you soon. And how are the rest of you?" She coolly glanced over Bernard, Prentiss, and Howard.

"Good. Just waiting on my ride," Bernard told her. "I came with Cyrus and he's still upstairs."

"Does Veronique know he's here?" Josephine asked, taking a seat with the men. "Do any of your wives know you're here?"

A pounding on the stairs made them turn around as Cyrus came rushing into the room. "Oh." He pulled up and straightened his blazer. "Madam, gentlemen. Ah, Madam, could I get a whiskey before I go?"

"Of course," Josephine went to the drinks cabinet and poured him a shot. "Cyrus. You all right?" She watched him knock it back. "Something happen?"

"No, no," he mumbled, fumbling in his pockets. "Just running a bit late is all."

"Late for what?" Bernard asked. "Are we ready to go?"

"In a minute." Cyrus held the glass out. "Can I get a refill?"

Josephine refilled the glass, adding more than what she'd first given him. "If there is something wrong, Cyrus, you need to tell me."

"No, no, Madam, not with you, or the girls. Just my personal life." He downed the drink and handed back the glass. "Thank you. I just received a phone call from ex-wife number one about the party the other week and the way I treated my children. I don't know why. I barely spoke to my sons. As you all know, I don't really care about my children in any way. Least of all my two daughters. Just like *their* mother, they are. The bitch."

"So why the phone call?" Howard wasn't fond of politicians, or lawyers, or cops, and barely tolerated them when he was there. Out in the real world, he didn't associate with them at all unless he was after something, such as money, or a favour.

"No idea. Especially this time of night." Cyrus glanced at his watch. "But then she lives on the west coast, so the time difference wouldn't matter to her. It was something about my treatment, and are they in the will, and have I disinherited them. Such nonsense. They were never in the will to begin with." He sagged into the chair evacuated by Josephine and sighed. "I never really cared for my children when they was born. But my wives kept pressuring me to make heirs, and that it would look good for my stature to be a family man. It would get me places, they both said. All it got me was endless nights of crying, diapers, pestering, and schooling. That's why I left it all to my exes. I didn't want those brats, so they could be the ones to look after them."

"But come time for photos to be taken of the great Cyrus Stratton, you gathered the family around and took the shots, right?" Bernard mocked. "Maybe you shouldn't have gotten married."

Cyrus nodded. "Maybe. I've seriously regretted it since I first did it. Maybe I should have just waited for Veronique."

"That's not to say she would have come along if you made different life choices and not married or had children." Josephine noted his pale expression and her ears perked up. She turned and saw Harlan sneaking down the stairs. "I'm surprised you come here. You own a men's magazine. Don't you have your own playground to fuck whores in?"

Harlan chuckled and smoothed out his royal blue velvet smoking jacket. "I do. But it's the thrill that brings me here."

"So, who else are we waiting on?" Josephine glanced at the grandfather clock. "And who wants a drink?"

*****

Bartholomew was downstairs in the black room. He'd bypassed the red room, and insisted on never using it again, especially since Josephine had allowed him to come back to see the girls.

She'd ordered that he never do to any other girl what he did to Harmony. He'd sworn up and down he wouldn't, and the darkness of the room suited his mood.

Heaven bounced up and down on his cock, and he tried grabbing her breasts, but they were just out of reach of his short arms.

"Damn it, I want to grope you," he growled, and grabbed her hips, pulling himself up. "I want your breasts."

Heaven kept bouncing. "Come on, Bartie, keep up. Here they are." She groped her breasts and pushed them towards him. "Suck on them."

He managed to get one in his mouth and sucked, inhaling as much as he could. It was ripe and delicious and tasted of the caviar he'd sucked off them earlier. He groaned in delight and fell backwards, taking her with him.

She adjusted herself and moved up and down his body so he could still get off and she could make this night be over. *It must be an hour already,* she thought. *When will this end?*

Bartie sucked greedily, coming inside of her while he did. "Oh," came out in a sigh. "That was good. It really is heaven being inside of you."

Heaven rolled her eyes and sat up. "It's almost an hour, Bartie. We just have time for a drink." She grabbed the champagne bottle from the ice bucket and finished off the few mouthfuls left. It was warm, but she didn't mind. It would help her get through the next few minutes.

*****

"I'll take a scotch," Harlan said, and took a seat on the rich green velvet couch. "Mind if I smoke?"

"Yes, I do." Josephine poured the drink and handed it over. "Anyone else?"

"I'll take a beer," Prentiss added. "I'm still waiting on Heaven. She's with Bartie."

Josephine bristled at the name. "Bloody Bartie Winthrop," she muttered. "I really should have banned him permanently." She rang for Fanny to bring a beer, and passed out drinks to the others. "I don't know why I let him back in after Harmony. I should have kicked him out in the cold and left him there."

"He paid his penance, didn't he?" Harlan downed his drink. "Told us all about it last month at the gentlemen's club Howard and I were taking a break at."

"Yes. I made sure to whip his pathetic white ass to the bone for what he'd done. I felt it necessary for punishment."

"Make him bleed, did you?" Prentiss asked before

finishing his beer.

"I most certainly did. But after everything else, I may just ban him after all."

"Where will the poor bastard go then?" Bernard asked. "And would it affect us?"

"Why would it affect us?" Cyrus pulled his phone from his pocket and saw Veronique's name. "I'm going to have to go shortly. The wife is calling."

"Which one?" the men asked in unison and sniggered.

"Veronique. But why would it affect us?" Cyrus slid his phone back into his pocket.

"Because," Bernard said, "if he does something stupid, *again*, and it gets out, the shit will hit the fan and we'll all be exposed. We keep this part of our life quiet. He needs to as well. For all our sakes."

*****

Heaven bounced away on Bartie's cock. "This is going to be the last time. Your hour is over and I need to get home."

"Just one more time." Bartie grunted, thrusting into her. "Roll over." He pushed her off and rolled her onto her stomach, coming in behind. "Yes, oh, yes." He pounded away as much as his weak legs could hold him up. His hand grasped her head, pushing it into the soft coverings while he leant on the other. He grunted to climax, unaware she was grasping at his hand on her head. "Oh, God, oh, God." His heart gave way and stopped.

Her hands fell to the bed.

He collapsed on top of her.

Chapter 4

Josephine glanced at the clock. "Heaven should be free now. Prentiss, which room were you meeting her in?"

"The blue room."

A gnawing feeling gripped her gut. Bartholomew Winthrop should never be left alone with a girl. "We need to go and check. Prentiss, come with me."

"Why?" he asked.

She paused in the doorway. "Because Bartie's overdue and you're an officer of the NYPD. I may need you. Come."

She led the way downstairs, with Prentiss following. And because the others were curious, they made a beeline after them.

Josephine barged right into the black room, flicked on the overhead light and gasped. Her hands flew to cover her mouth and she was shoved aside as Prentiss dashed to the bed.

He checked for Bartie's pulse and shook his head. "Dead." He rolled him off Heaven. "Damn. I was meant to be with her next." He rolled her over and felt her neck. "No pulse."

"Do something," Josephine cried. "CPR, something."

Prentiss tried it on Heaven for several minutes to no avail. "It's not happening, Madam, sorry."

"God fucking damn it," Josephine screamed, her hands clenched by her sides. "He's fucking killed another one. What the fuck do we do now?" She wildly looked at every man standing in the room. Bigwig politicians, a cop, a director, a producer, and a men's magazine publisher. "What the fuck do we do now?"

They silently stood there, looking at each other, looking at Bartie and Heaven, looking at Josephine, fear and trepidation in their eyes and on their faces.

What they had feared upstairs had now happened.

Prentiss sighed and crawled off the bed. "I'll deal with Heaven's body, as I did with Harmony. And we have to figure out what we're doing with Bartie."

"Dump his body where you dump Heaven's," Josephine said scathingly. "Where you dumped Harmony's. Wherever the hell it is that no one but you knows about. Or leave his body out on the road, or in the park, or wherever it's going to be found so he can be shamed in death."

"His office," Bernard suggested.

"His home," Donald added.

"His wife would know." Harlan tightened the cord on his jacket. "The bastard took us out."

"Is his wife still alive?" Prentiss asked. "I could take his body to his office, but it's very public. Does he have a house somewhere that's not his residence?"

"What do you mean?" Cyrus stared at the two bodies. Even in death Heaven had great tits and he'd never tried them out.

"If he lives here in the city, does he have a place on Long Island, in the Hamptons, or upstate New York where he would go for a break?" Prentiss pushed on. "If I dump him where he can't be found, then the Press will have a field day with why he disappeared. If I dump him in his home somewhere, he can be found and the autopsy will show a heart attack, or whatever the hell it is he had."

Josephine stared at the bodies with remorse. She had allowed him back. Allowed him to be alone. And now she'd lost another girl. "Dump him in plain sight. Let the Press go wild on why he's found naked somewhere public. You know where the cameras are, so bypass them to make it happen. I don't care if it's here or upstate, or Long Island. Dump him where he can be found and humiliated for all to see."

The men exchanged silent glances, hoping her wrath never extended to them.

"But what happens if he is found?" Cyrus quietly asked. "What if he's somehow connected back to us?"

Josephine sent her scathing gaze at him. "*You* are a politician, Cyrus, as is Bernard. Prentiss is a cop, you can all make sure whatever investigation is started can be kept private, or stopped completely. I want him to be humiliated in death. I don't care how you cover it up. Just make sure it doesn't come back to any of us."

Bernard and Cyrus glanced at each other and nodded.

"We can do something if the time arises," Bernard said. "Meanwhile, Prentiss, what is your plan?"

"Don't have one, so we'd better come up with one." He looked to Josephine. "Madam? Your call."

"Why's it her call?" Harlan complained. "We're all

going to be dumped in it."

"Not if we do as she suggested," Prentiss snapped. "Bernard and Cyrus can ask for the case to be closed. I can say they asked me personally to look for him."

"Why would they go to you?" Donald asked. "Specifically, you."

"Because I'm a lieutenant and I'm in the same precinct as Bartie. I've gone before him in cases before. We're from the same area. They wanted—"

"Do you go running?" Josephine sagged onto the chair by the wall.

Prentiss furrowed his brow. "Yeah, why?"

"Do you go running any place that would make it easy to find his body? The park, the courthouse, his house?"

Prentiss got her drift. "Yeah, I do. I can be the one to discover the body on my run."

"Then make it happen." She nodded. "Humiliate him and make sure to cover your ass. Make sure to cover all of our asses." She paused and looked around the room at two dead bodies; clothes strewn around. "You're going to need gloves. Don't leave evidence. Everyone else can get out." She slowly rose to her feet and waved them off. With a last glance at Heaven, she hustled out the door to gather what they needed.

The rest of the men gathered outside the sex room.

"We should go. Then we won't know what happens," Cyrus said. "I'll call my driver."

"And I'll call mine." Harlan pulled out his phone and made the call. "On his way. We should be out of here before Prentiss takes the body."

They silently watched Josephine return with gloves

and plastic body bags and walk into the room.

Just as silently, she and Prentiss gloved up and put Heaven into a body bag, as they had done with Harmony. Then, they rolled Bartie into a bag.

"And his clothes?" she asked watching Prentiss zip up the bag.

"Burn them. Or I can bury them with Heaven." Prentiss pulled off his gloves. "I can transport him and dump him out of the bag when I get there. Then I can pretend to run past and find him. They won't find evidence, except maybe semen or vaginal samples, but they'll have no one to match it back to. I'll have to check the maps to find the best spot without cameras, and figure out where to park."

"I don't want to know." Josephine waved him off. "The less I know, the better, but I'll wait to see it all on the news tomorrow."

"Probably for the next few months." Prentiss grabbed an extra pair of gloves and held them up. "For later."

She nodded, a sigh escaping her lips. The black of the room did nothing but drag the mood down. No one would be using this room until it was repainted. It needed an overhaul, just as the red room had. Now it was technically a rose colour, not flaming red as it had been, after a makeover following Harmony's death.

Now she had Heaven *and* Bartie's deaths to deal with.

God knew what the hell was going to come from this.

*****

The next day, Josephine awaited the news. She had banned

the men for a month, and already called in the painters and removalists to strip the room. She wanted no reminders of Bartie or Heaven. She had also called up everyone due to come in and rebooked them. She needed a couple of days off to digest it all.

She scoured the five local newspapers for any word, but there was nothing. She had the TV on in the library, but there was nothing.

Until the evening news.

"Breaking news tonight. The body of New York judge Bartholomew Winthrop has been found naked at the far end of Central Park. A local officer, out for his early morning run, discovered the body and called it in. The judge's body was taken to the morgue for examination, and his family called. All of his cases have been stopped due to his death and will be rescheduled with other judges."

She sighed. That was that. Dead and naked. Served him right.

*****

The coroner took swabs from Bartie's body and set them side by side on his tray. He'd photographed it already, and was about to do the autopsy next. He made a note of the healed welts and bruises on his paperwork, then picked up his scalpel.

An hour later he was stitching up Bartie's body.

"Doc."

Michael Cullen looked up in surprise. "Mr Mayor. What are you doing here?"

Allen slowly walked over to the table. "I thought I would come and make sure Bartie was being treated with the utmost care. The citizens of this state are worried that one of our own has been murdered."

"Not necessarily murdered." Michael cut the thread and lay down his tools. "Examination shows a massive heart attack, clogged arteries, and diabetes. He was a walking talking dead man."

Allen appraised the coroner and chose his words carefully. "So, he died of natural causes?"

"Looks like it." Michael pulled off his gloves and dumped them in the bin. "My report will be done by morning."

"But what about the fact he was found naked in the park?" Allen asked, staring down at Bartie all white and dead.

"No idea. That's one for the cops. Maybe he went skinny dipping in the pond, or a nearby pool, and ran away when he thought someone was coming. Had a heart attack and fell down dead." Michael covered the body and removed his gown, throwing it in the bin after the gloves. "Not much else I can tell you, Mayor."

Allen spied the tray of swab sticks. "Did you find anything on the body to indicate he'd been swimming?"

"Not yet. I'll send the swabs off to forensics and see what they come up with. Could be a delay though."

"Tell them to push it through on the word of the mayor." Allen lifted the sheet to look at Bartie one last time. "What the hell were you doing, you stupid old fool?"

*****

At the gentlemen's club, the place was abuzz with the news. Gossip and rumours abounded, floating from table, to lounge, to table of politicians, lawyers, other judges and bigwigs.

Bartie Winthrop had been found dead and naked in Central Park.

Whatever was next?

Harlan glanced around and leant in to the men seated around the coffee table. "We need to keep this to ourselves," he said in a low voice. "No one speaks to anyone unless they have to, and then declare that you know nothing."

The men nodded.

"So what if the cops want to speak to us?" Cyrus asked. "Bernard and I are politicians."

Harlan let out a sigh. "I just told you, Cyrus. Say nothing unless you have to. But I seriously doubt you'll need to. None of us will unless the Press, or cops, know we knew Bartie personally."

"Well, we did." Bernard sipped his bourbon. "Cyrus and I both did."

"Whereas Donald and I didn't." Howard glanced slyly over at the table full of other judges. "But they all did. Wonder how many see madams on the regular and knew he did too. They should be the ones who are scared of their wives and the Press finding out."

"Wonder how many saw MX?" Donald grinned and sipped his cognac. "Won't those interviews be a laugh a minute."

"I seriously doubt that's a scandal any of them would want." Harlan finished his brandy and held up his glass for the waiter to see. It was promptly replaced by a fresh drink, and he waited for the waiter to walk away. "I have a feeling this is going to be swept under the carpet very quickly."

"Considering he was a judge, and found naked, it would have to be." Howard nodded, and watched the judges. "Many, many lives and careers are now at stake."

"Let's hope ours are not," Cyrus said and glanced at his watch. "I need to head out. Veronique will be waiting."

"Unless she's banging her sidepiece." Harlan chuckled and stared at the shock raining down over Cyrus's bright red face. "Or didn't you know?"

Cyrus stuttered, "Wha-what?"

"Oh," Harlan murmured. "How do you not know your wife is banging the pool boy? Last year it was the gardener, or didn't you find out why she had suddenly let him go and hired a new one. An *old* one. Yep." Harlan chuckled. "Pool boy's next to be replaced."

Cyrus breathed to calm his jittering nerves. "Well… I…"

"Give up the charade," Harlan told him. "You must've known. Just as I reckon she knows you're off seeing someone on the side. Except in your case, it's a madam and her whores. In hers, it's the men hired to keep your garden trimmed. Which is exactly what he would've done to her garden. Kept it trimmed."

"Do you have to be so damn vulgar?" Cyrus sputtered and stormed to his feet. "You're a sick pervert, Harlan Conway." Aware that all eyes were now on him, he calmly made his way out of the club and into his limousine.

Harlan laughed and downed another drink. "He always was so weak and lily-livered."

Donald and Howard glanced at each other and finished off their drinks.

"Time for me to go as well." Donald called his limo driver. "I'll be out in a moment. Harlan, Bernard, Howard. See you next time."

"I'll come with you." Howard stood up and straightened his blazer. "Time to be heading off."

"Lily-livered gutless cowards," Harlan hissed and crossed his legs. He glanced at Bernard. "You going too?"

Bernard checked his watch. "I'd better. It's late and I'm done for the day. I'll walk you gentleman out." He sent a scathing glare Harlan's way. "Harlan, running a men's magazine has certainly done you no favours with manners. Learn some."

The three men walked away, leaving Harlan scowling at all of them.

*****

Police Commissioner Cormac Ryan was called into the mayor's office a day later.

"Cormac, take a seat. Tell me, what's going on with the Bartholomew Winthrop case." Allen sat behind his desk and waited for Cormac to sit. "I want to know the details. Every detail. From the reports to the officer who found him."

Cormac sighed and settled in. "There's not much to tell." He grasped his hands together in front of him. "Lieutenant Adler was out for his morning run around the park when he came across the body and called it in. The judge was taken to the morgue and the crime scene unit did a thorough search of the area. So far, we have no idea why he was there, or where his clothes and ID are."

Allen nodded, pursing his lips in thought. He'd suspected Bartie might have died at Madam X's, and a phone call to her on his private line had confirmed it. She'd told him it had taken care of it and that she'd wanted Bartie humiliated for it. All of this was something Allen did not want coming out in case it affected his re-election as mayor. "Okay. This lieutenant…is he a good egg? A good cop? Straight and to the point?"

"Absolutely." Cormac nodded. "A pristine record, several commendations and awards, gets along well with his team."

"Good, good." Allen leant back in his chocolate brown leather desk chair and swivelled towards the floor-to-ceiling window in his office. It afforded him a skyline view of the city. "I want this to be kept as private as possible. Out of the Press…if possible. Well..." He sighed. "As much as possible. For his family's sake. I've already called his wife and given my condolences, as I'm sure many others have. But this is something I don't want to take long. It needs to be kept on the downlow so the rest of the judges can feel safe."

"They don't now?" Cormac studied the mayor's face. While they rarely got along and didn't agree on most things, this was something they *could* agree on.

"Well," Allen huffed and turned back to his desk. "Considering a judge was found dead and naked in Central Park, they're all feeling a little worried about whether or not this is the start of something against judges or law enforcement in general. When we spoke, I told them to up their security and stay safe. Don't take chances…don't stay out late at night."

"Wise words," Cormac said. "Is that all?"

Allen stared at Cormac for a few moments. "Is what all?"

Cormac's thick brown brows rose. "Is that all you wanted to see me about?"

"Oh, yes. Just about the horrible death of Judge Winthrop. Stay on the case and see to it personally that it's kept quiet. Mary, his wife, is preparing his funeral. I suggested she keep it private and out of the Press. She said she was going to invite all of his friends, but I suggested not to, especially as we didn't know if this was a one-off, a simple heart attack, or if there's a killer targeting judges." He sighed. "She said she'd see."

"It's a reasonable idea to keep it private, because no, we don't know who or what the killer is, or whether they're after judges or not, or even if there *is* a killer. I'll keep on it. Now…is *that* all?"

Allen nodded and swivelled back to the window. "Thanks for coming in, Cormac. I knew you'd see it my way."

Dismissed, Cormac rose and ambled out the door. It closed behind him and he paused. *See what his way?*

*****

Josephine ambled around her brownstone. She had dismissed the girls for the week, and informed the gentlemen in question that they were not to come. This entire fiasco had made her more aware of how limited time was. *Her* time was. The status of the men who came to see her girls could cause real harm if they banded together and blamed her. But she had her secret weapons prepared and ready to go. And if she had to use them to get her way and keep her life secret, she would.

They didn't need the truth coming to light. Their dirty little habits and proclivities needed to stay hidden away from the prying eyes of the Press, their peers, and their wives.

She sighed and sat on the chair in the front window of the parlour. The last few weeks had been trying; more so than any other period in her life. Her mother's life was a different story. So was her grandmother's. But since she'd taken over the business, there had been no problems because the men who came to her wanted it all kept a secret. The problem with secrets, though, was that many of them came to light. She had taken precautions to make sure she had evidence of those secrets and if anything untoward came to pass, she would be using it. And now something *might* happen, thanks to Bartie Winthrop.

"The fools have no idea what I have on them, and if they did know, hell would be paid." She sat back and crossed her slender legs, smoothing the long, soft blue woollen dress over her knees. When she wasn't working, in either Madam X mode, or as mistress of the house, she dressed in a very simple fashion. No Victorian era dresses, no leather and no whips. Just simple, but fashionable dresses and low heels. Her grey hair hung down her back, held with a headband of pale blue velvet. Simple small silver studs in the shape of a flower adorned her lobes. They were a gift from her mother, passed down from her grandmother. An old Cartier silver watch with diamonds wrapped around her wrist, and her mother's and grandmother's rings adorned her right hand.

That was Josephine Pompadour. Simple and casual. Not dressed up like a Christmas turkey every day. Only every night that gentlemen callers came round.

Her foot swung slightly as she thought about Bartie and every man who had passed through her basement door. Always the basement door, as none of them had to the balls to face it head on and walk through her front door. They always had to hide. Stay hidden from the public eye. Never be seen.

"What to do, what to do," she muttered. "What do I do if this blows back on me?"

"Ma'am?" Hilda came into the room. "Would you like something to eat or drink?"

Josephine glanced at the clock. It was only one in the afternoon. "No, thank you, Hilda. I'll wait until dinnertime."

"But you haven't eaten since breakfast." Hilda wrung her hands in front of her. "You need to eat. You didn't eat much breakfast—a piece of toast and a cup of tea is nothing."

"It's enough for me." Josephine gave her a small smile. "I'm getting on in years and eating less and less. Besides, I'm not hungry. Too much to think about."

"Anything I can do, ma'am?" Hilda stepped closer, always on the ready to help her mistress, but never close enough to overstep the mark if not needed.

"No, thank you, Hilda. You go back to what you were doing. Or take an early mark and go and do something else. Visit a market, or go shopping."

Hilda brightened. "Oh, thank you, ma'am. I do need to buy presents for my grandchildren."

"Then go and do it. Come back when you feel like it."

"Thank you, ma'am. I'll go and change. Is there anything you want or need?"

Josephine laughed. "There's a lot, but nothing you can help me with. Go and have fun. I'll see you later. Take Fanny or Myrtle with you if they want to go."

"Will you be okay here on your own?"

"I will. I'll call you a cab." She did that while Hilda went off to change and speak to Fanny and Myrtle. The cab arrived just as Hilda and Fanny hurried downstairs.

"We're off, ma'am. See you later. Myrtle's not feeling well and is lying down, but she'll get you anything you need."

"No need, I'm quite capable of doing things for myself. I hope you find everything you're after," Josephine called as Hilda and Fanny rushed down the stoop stairs for the cab. She waited until they'd closed the back door before locking up the house.

The phone rang out in the quiet, making her jump.

She tsked, and hurried for the phone. "Hello, Josephine Pompadour's residence."

"It's Allen Gerard. Can we talk?"

"Of course, Mr Mayor. How may I help you."

"I've spoken to the commissioner, and several other judges. The case is being kept quiet and out of the Press. I've also spoken to Bartie's wife. She's planning a funeral for him this weekend. And while I've suggested she keep it private, she insists on it being an open service for his friends to attend."

"Will you be there?"

"Of course. As will other judges, I'm sure." He paused. "Will you?"

Josephine chuckled. "While I may have been up in the ranks of high society once upon a time, I'm not any more. Not for the last few decades. But…" She thought about it. "Who knows what I'll decide to do come the weekend. Where's his funeral?"

"At St Patrick's Cathedral."

"Interesting choice of venue," she murmured. "In the end, I hated the man. His proclivities murdered two of my girls and their families will never know that. They will never know their daughters, granddaughters, sisters, aunts are dead. Maybe I should go so I can laugh in his face."

"Would you really?" Allen perfectly understood how she felt. He was shocked to have found out Bartie had killed the poor girl in such a manner, but never thought it would come so close to home; the home of the madam to the half of New York who serviced the other half of New York.

"Yes, I probably would. I'm glad the bastard's dead. Serves him right. As for his wife, I knew her a long time ago. Cold bitch she was and probably still is. She can't be surprised that her husband was found in such a way. She also shouldn't be surprised if she finds out he was seeing a madam and whores. I wonder if she ever questioned why he was covered in welts."

"Probably not since they hadn't been living together in four years." Allen, brushed the crumbs from his pastrami on rye from his lap. He was eating at his desk, not wanting to be seen in public during this time.

"Four years," Josephine murmured. "Interesting. Maybe I *should* attend, then."

"Just to cause trouble?"

"Trouble? Who, me?"

"Be careful, Madam Pompadour. That trouble may come home to roost one day."

Chapter 5

The funeral of Bartholomew Winthrop was held at St Patrick's Cathedral on Fifth Avenue, and it was quite the show.

Every row was packed with people coming to pay their respects, and with standing room only, many loitered at the back and around the sides. Judges, lawyers, the mayor and the commissioner joined cops, politicians, and hangers-on who all wanted to bid him farewell to the other side.

Mary Winthrop, Bartie's stoic estranged wife, sat in the front pew, dabbing her eyes with her black lace hanky. Neck to toe in black, she cut a miserable figure in the church. There were no children to sit with her, no parents or siblings. She was alone, as Bartie had been, in life as single children. Both had decided to not have any, and lived their lives for Bartie's legal needs. He wanted to be a judge, and by God he was going to be one and not let children get in the way.

Mary had agreed, not wanting children herself. Or, at least, not with Bartie. She had given birth at thirteen, when a boy she had fancied took his advances too far and against her will. Her parents had forced her to have the baby and give it up, not caring that she'd been the victim of an assault, and had then shipped her off to her grandmother's for a strict upbringing and education.

And while she had often wondered about her son at the time, she lost her memories of the horrid event to the point she'd completely forgotten she'd given birth all those years ago. But every now and then, when the subject of children would crop up in her women's circles and groups, a vague memory of giving birth to a boy came back to her. The memory of the pain and her screaming, of him screaming and being taken away… In those brief moments, she wondered if he was still alive, if he'd had a good or a bad life, and if he'd made something of himself. Maybe he'd become a politician, a lawyer or judge. Hell, he could even be a criminal. She wondered where he lived, if he'd had a family, if he knew he'd been taken away by force and given to someone else.

In the first few years, she'd thought about what it would have been like to raise him, to be his mother, to have a son, a child while she was still a child herself, but in the years since her marriage, she'd grown to hope he never came to light to ruin her husband's career, and her very rich and luxurious lifestyle.

Is that lifestyle going to end now? she thought, staring at her husband's coffin at the front of the church. *What if he came back? What if my son came back now? Would I want him? Would I need him? Would I be lonely enough to accept him into my life? He'd be fifty-seven or so now. Could I deal with being a mother to a man I don't know and never had the chance to be a parent to?*

Could he have children of his own? Could I have grandchildren? Could they take the place of Bartie? Maybe I should finally track him down… Maybe, once I get back to Los Angeles. But Bartie's dead and gone, so do I really need someone else to take care of in my life? Maybe, he just needs to stay gone.

Bartie had an open coffin, for all to pass after the service and before he was removed for burial. She had wanted it that way as a reminder to all who had supported him, and in turn, supported her. Because she would need it now. At seventy, she had lived a lavish lifestyle on Bartie's income. It would no longer be coming in, but she had his retirement fund to live on instead. She would be selling their New York homes, an Upper East Side brownstone, and a Hampton's mansion, so she could continue to live the life of luxury in Beverly Hills where she had been residing in the warmth of the balmy sunshine for the last four years. She needed the money, and she hoped Bartie had not changed his will since their separation.

She'd also wondered what he'd been up to these last four years. On occasion she had hired a detective agency to watch him. He had frequented another brownstone on the Upper East Side regularly, secretively arriving and leaving by the garage.

It was owned by Josephine Pompadour, and it had been suggested in the detective's notes, that while once a society woman, she was now living the life of a madam and brothel keeper.

Mary had been shocked, but once that wore off she'd realised this was nothing new for her husband. She had figured out he'd been to one or two during their marriage, as sexual encounters had been few and far between in their bedroom. After meeting him and his proposing, she'd refused him and told him why after he hounded her.

He told her he didn't care, that he had a penchant for whips and chains, and if she couldn't do it for him, he'd find someone who could. Her new money status was what he was after.

Mary thought back to her twenties. Ten years after the assault and birth, she had graduated with honours from college, and bought stocks with an up-and-coming company with the money she had saved over ten years doing drudge work, determined to make something of herself, while she was pushed through school by her hateful and extremely religious abusive grandmother. And she did make something of herself. She had her degree in economics and business, and knew what she was doing. That was why she left home the moment she could.

Ten years later, on her thirty-third birthday to be exact, those stocks paid off big time, making her a millionaire. Her grandmother demanded half for putting up with her all those years. Mary finally had the emotional strength to tell her to go to hell and slapped her grandmother across the face. Her grandmother reeled backward in shock, and promptly had a heart attack and died. Mary walked out the door, never to be seen in that house again, and left that life behind. She didn't even go back for the reading of the will. Nothing was left to her anyway, so what would be the point. She cashed in half of her stocks, kept half for a retirement fund, and put herself out to the world.

That's when she caught the eye of Bartholomew Winthrop at the local dance for high society. As an up-and-coming lawyer who had also purchased stocks in the same company, Bartie had always claimed it was love at first sight.

Love on Bartie's part; liking on Mary's. She wasn't interested in being in love, sex, or marriage, but knew his hard working enthusiasm for his job would take him far. Especially if she backed him.

Once she told him the truth, his truth came to light. And in the dead of the night, they made a pact to wed and support each other with their business and political endeavours without having to consummate a loveless marriage.

Of course, people questioned why children never appeared. Mary fobbed it off and Bartie told them to mind their own business.

And here they were, in the church, with Mary getting set to bury her husband in legal name only, and take everything he owned and she felt she deserved.

Mary gazed over her shoulder and wondered who was there. She spied a few faces she knew, nodded, and her gaze moved on. She saw other judges, and turned slightly in her seat. A few lawyers were there, people she had invited to dinner over the years, cops and the mayor. She nodded to Allen and turned around further. Her gaze moved on and came to rest on a women in flaming red. Sitting at the back of the church, in the last pew, the woman wore a Victorian era velvet dress with a low bodice, her chest adorned with a red stone necklace. Red plumage decorated her upswept grey hair, and she stared defiantly back at Mary.

Mary blinked, realised who she was, and quickly turned to the front, her heart hammering with anger in her chest. *How dare she turn up here. How dare she wear red. How goddamn fucking dare she!*

Mary's thoughts were interrupted by the priest taking the pulpit, and for the next hour, they sang hymns, read prayers, and spoke about Bartholomew Winthrop.

When the service came to an end, Mary turned in her seat. The woman was gone. Her gaze darted around the church, but she couldn't find her.

"And now, we will have the procession where you can all come past and pay your respects to Judge Winthrop," the priest said, looking over the crowd. "From my left, we will start with the front row and go row from row to make things easier…" His gaze landed on the woman in red who was standing off to the side in front of the first row.

Josephine waltzed up the stairs and over to Bartie's coffin with not a care in the world, knowing full well every eye in that room was on her.

Silence fell over the church and not one sound was heard. Every man who knew who she was held his breath; every person who didn't, wasn't there. For every man in that church knew exactly who Josephine Pompadour was and had, at one time, been serviced by her or one of her girls.

Josephine laid her right hand on the edge of the coffin. "Bartie, you old cunt. So glad you got your comeuppance. You killed two of my girls."

Mary slowly rose to her feet and walked up the stairs to her husband and his whore. "What are you doing here?"

she muttered close to Josephine's ear. "You aren't welcome."

"None of us are. It was an open invitation," Josephine replied, her gaze on Bartie's face, seeing that the welt from the whip was covered up with make-up. "Mary, holding up well for an old girl. Still a bitch, I see." She finally moved her gaze to the wife. "Did they have a problem with the welts on his back?"

Mary's head sharply pulled back. "Those were from you?"

"Of course." Josephine smiled. "How else do you think he got his dick hard? Certainly not married to a woman like you. Besides, I also know you hired a detective to follow him and found me. I know *him very well.*" Her gaze travelled up and down Mary's floor length black dress. "In mourning, how gauche. You didn't love him any more than he loved you."

"At least I'm showing my respect for the tradition, unlike you, coming dressed like a harlot," Mary spat, no longer caring who heard. "The slut from Russia with her call girls. Just like your mother."

Josephine's gloved hand swept across Mary's face, sending her back a couple of steps and holding her cheek while gasps rang out around the church. "And how many people know you gave birth at thirteen to a bastard child?" She said it loud enough for the first few rows, and the priest, who reeled back in shock, to hear. "Check your morals, Mary Winthrop, you frigid bitch. We all know your marriage to Bartie was one of convenience and not love. It was purely for the politics of law and society. You both used each other." She saw several men rising from their seats and raised her voice. "It's funny how men will tell their concubines everything in the throes of sexual release. It's also just as well I have it all on record." Her comment levelled every man on his feet back into his seat. "If only Bartie had kept his pants up. Mary, I hope you rot in hell alongside him. He deserved the ending he got." With a rustle of her dress, Josephine Pompadour, madam to every man in that church, swept down the nave and out the door without a backward glance.

After a long, nervous silence, murmurs appeared.

Mary slowly dropped her hand, her face flaming red at the performance. While Josephine was right, it didn't mean she'd ever wanted it to be made public. Pulling herself together, she moved to the side of the coffin and smoothed her husband's blazer. She had chosen his navy blue, with a matching set of tie and blue pocket kerchief. "If only I could kill you myself, Bartie, you bastard. If only you hadn't gone to see that Russian slut. Maybe you'd still be alive." She paused and took a breath. "But then again, maybe it was time for you to be gone, after all. Can't say I'm sad to see you go. I only wanted your money and prestige and what it provided." She breathed in and settled her nerves before stepping over to the priest to stand guard over the coffin while the procession happened.

She watched every man in that room walk past, look in on Bartie, mutter a few words, give their respects to her, and then walk down the nave.

She wondered if Josephine was outside, waiting to see what happened. She wondered if she'd be able to deal with another encounter with her. She sighed, plastered a fake smile on her face, and nodded at the condolences.

Outside, Josephine sat in the back seat of her town car watching the parade of men leave the church. She knew it had been risky revealing such a detail, but she'd wanted to make sure they all knew what they were up against if they tried blaming her.

They could also be tempted to not come back to her abode for their pleasure, but at this point of her life, she didn't really care. She had enough to money to live well for the next twenty plus years, and could easily leave the business behind after this.

She sighed, and watched Cormac and Allen leave the church, deep in conversation. She knew it was about her. It couldn't be about anyone else when the mayor and police commissioner left a church together after her performance. All of them were deep in thought as they strode to their cars, no doubt wondering what was going to happen now.

"I'll soon know," she muttered. "No doubt cancellations will start coming thick and fast. Wonder if any death threats will arise? It'll make for interesting conversations next time they come." She continued watching until the coffin was carried to the hearse, loaded into the back, and the back door was shut. She watched as Mary slid into a limousine, and the procession take off.

"No family, no friends. She didn't have friends either? Why is no one with her? Interesting." Josephine stared in thought out the open window, chin resting on her hand as her elbow leant on the car handle. "No one is here for her. They're all here for Bartie, may he rot in hell."

The other back door opened and she jumped in surprise

as Cormac entered the car and slammed the door shut.

"Josephine."

"Cormac, you scared me." She leant forward to her driver. "Rocco, was that door not locked?"

"Ah…" He blushed. "Obviously not. Sorry, ma'am."

Josephine settled back. "Cormac. To what do I owe the pleasure?"

"What the hell was that display?" he demanded. "What the hell gave you the right to disgrace the legacy of the judge and his wife? What the hell gave you any right to be there, dressed in red…" He perused her outfit. "And to make a spectacle of yourself and embarrass Mary?"

"Oh, please," she scoffed. "There was no spectacle, and there sure as hell is no legacy. When you dig down into Bartie's life he was an asshole with fetishes his precious wife was never going to fulfil. I came to pay my respects."

Cormac shifted and adjusted the left side of his blazer. "That was uncalled for, uncouth, and unnecessary. And what was that line about having it all on record?"

"Yes." She smiled smugly. "I did notice that those of you who had risen to come and get me suddenly dropped back into your seats. It's a warning, Cormac. Bartie killed two of my girls and he himself died in the throes. All of you have given me much ammunition to use in case I need to. This will not blow back on me. You will either leave me alone, or keep all of this on the quiet. In fact, I really don't mind if you all find another madam to be serviced by. Things need to change, and I no longer want dead girls on my hands. And if their families come looking for them, what will *you* tell them?"

Cormac stared at her, deep in thought. "What *can I* tell them? That they worked for a madam. I don't even know what you're talking about. What dead girls?"

Josephine arched her head back. "The two girls of mine that Bartie killed in the throes of ejaculation. One of your own dealt with the bodies, and a lawyer went along with it. When Bartie decided to also keel over, that officer dealt with it and everyone else there went along with it. There are witnesses; there are participants. I'm not the only one who had to deal with the fallout of Bartie's stupidity. Maybe it's time for me to shut down my business and retire." She settled back and sighed. "Maybe it's time for all of us to retire from our professions and move on before any more die in the throes of passion."

"Two girls died by Bartie's hand?" Cormac asked. "One of my officer's dealt with it? And a lawyer knows what happened."

"As if you don't know who comes to the brownstone to see me. I have a feeling you may know many, many members of my exclusive club, having been one yourself." Josephine looked at the car across the road. It had been there since the funeral, and contained the mayor. "Allen's watching. He's waiting for you to threaten me, is he?"

"Why would you say that?"

"I saw you walk out together, deep in conversation. Not going to the cemetery? I wonder who is."

"I never want it known that I used your services, do you understand me?"

She peered at him under hooded lids. "Or your father, or three of your sons. The exploits seem to also be inherited, like those sapphire blue eyes and wavy brown hair."

A mix of fear and anger thundered across his face. "Don't you ever think you can threaten me or my family. I won't stand for it."

"Who's threatening?" she asked. "Merely stating a fact. And careful, Cormac. I've kept everyone's secrets so far, that's part of my job, but with Bartie dying a murderer, things are getting dicey, for *everyone* involved. That includes you, *and* the mayor. Tell him that. That Bartie's death may full well be the catalyst for change and you can blame Bartie for that. As for the families of the girls, I have no idea who they are, or where they are, but if they come looking to the cops for answers or to find them, what are you going to do? Two girls are dead; Harmony wanted to be a veterinarian and nearly had her degree. What will you do if the family comes calling on your doorstep?"

Cormac sighed. "Nothing. Because I have no idea who they are or what they did. But if you're not careful, Josephine, I may just send them your way." He opened the car door and set his foot on the pavement.

"And I will send them right to you," she replied. "Good day, Cormac. Tell Allen not to worry. Everyone's secrets are safe with me. So far…"

The car door slammed shut and she watched Cormac walk across the road and get into the mayor's car. "Cheeky bastard. Going from my car to his. Telling tales on me to Allen. Naughty, naughty."

*****

"What did she say?"

Cormac settled. "Claimed she'll keep our secrets safe, so far. As long as we leave her alone and make no mention of Bartie or the girls."

"Girls? What girls?"

"The two whores he killed in the throes of passion. Apparently, one of my officers dealt with it, a lawyer knows about it, as do others that were there at the time."

"Wait, what?" Allen swiped his hands over his face, pretending he knew nothing. "Bartie killed two girls during the act? Fucking hell. And one of your officers knows? Who? Did she say?"

"No, but I'd say it's the one who found him. Officer Prentiss Adler."

"How? Why? What the fuck!" Allen leant back and breathed. "What the fuck, Cormac? Bartie killed two girls, and Josephine and others covered it up?"

"From what she said, I gather that's what happened. But knowing all of this, and knowing he's dead and now buried, I'm hesitant to make something out of it. If everyone keeps it to themselves, we should be safe. Her comment to Mary was a warning shot to all of us. She has proof of us being there, but won't use it if she's left alone. We're safe, if *she's* safe."

Allen shook his head and stared out through the tinted bullet-proof glass of his window. "Then I guess we'd better stay quiet. And I guess we'd better stop going to her—"

"Not that I was," Cormac cut in.

"Yeah, well," Allen huffed. "I hadn't seen her in a while, but I will certainly *not* be going back."

"I don't think many men will, now she's proclaimed

that she has evidence of promiscuity. Imagine if that all came out."

Allen gazed thoughtfully at him. "Are you saying she needs to be removed?"

Cormac gazed back. "I said no such thing."

"She needs to be removed…" Allen thought about it. "If Madam X was no longer in the public realm, we would all be safer."

"But the men who visit other madams and prostitutes would not be. Are you asking me to arrest her, or murder her?"

"If we arrest her, it could all come out. If she's…taken out, then we'll have the ability to search her house for the evidence."

"And if she doesn't have it at the house?"

Allen cocked his head. "We'll find it. We just have to figure out a way of getting her out of our hair."

"If she's arrested, then she'll expect the judge, the lawyer, the whomever, to set her free because of that evidence."

"Maybe. Either way, I suggest we keep having this discussion another time. I'm famished. See you again, Cormac."

"Mayor." Cormac alighted and went to his own car.

Allen pulled out his phone and called a number. "We need to deal with this."

*****

At the gentlemen's club on Fifth, everyone else gathered to farewell Bartie.

Harlan, Howard, Donald, Dirk, Bernard, Cyrus, Benedict,

along with other judges and lawyers who knew him, and those who didn't.

Cyrus held his glass aloft. "To Bartie. He was an asshole, and thank God he's gone, and now we don't have to worry about him killing off MX's girls."

"To Bartie," their small group cheered. With the sound of the other cheers and conversation going on, no one had heard theirs.

They drank in silence for a moment.

"I'm glad the old bastard's gone." Harlan put his drink down to pull out a Cuban cigar. He ran it under his nose to take in the rich aromas, before clipping the end and lighting it, taking his time to inhale the first few sucks. No one spoke until he was done.

"So am I," Cyrus added. "He was nothing but trouble in the end. Trouble."

"With a capital T." Howard languished in his wingback leather chair. "After what he did, if only the rest of the mugs in this room knew they wouldn't be celebrating his life."

"Like we just did," Donald replied, arching a brow. "Seriously, Howard, the man is dead, there is no need to celebrate it, or be thankful for it. What's done is done."

"Did you hear what Josephine said to Mary? I was too far away, but you were in the second row, Benedict. What was it?" Cyrus asked.

Benedict's gaze darted around the room and he leaned in to tell them the whole sordid conversation. "I'm worried she's serious. What if she does?"

"What *if* she does?" Harlan asked. "Would it be so wrong for her to have it? As long as we keep our mouths shut, she keeps her mouth shut. Right? Tit for tat, and all that. It's not like some of us haven't taken photos or videos of us doing it with the girls."

The others looked at him in disgust.

"You what?" Howard asked. "You've taken photos and videos? When? Who? Why wouldn't you do that in your own filthy grotto?"

Harlan's chuckle was dry and rough. "Please, like you all haven't. Two can play the game, and Josephine will keep on allowing me in as long as I have my own proof. Bedsides," he waved a hand, "she wasn't serious. She knows what would happen if we all suddenly stopped going."

"Did you see what she was wearing?" Donald asked. "That was a hell of a dress. Wonder if it was new."

"She did look stunning, for a funeral." Harlan sucked back on his Cuban. "Always looks fabulous when she's dressed up. And after what she said to Mary, did you see Mary's face? And that slap! I wish I'd been filming it for the magazine."

"Was that *really* necessary?" Bernard sipped his scotch. "Right in front of everyone her hand whipped across poor Mary's face. *In a church. At a funeral.* Whatever was she thinking?"

"That Mary had just called her a Russian slut, just like her mother. No wonder Josephine slapped her." Cyrus waved for another drink. "That was quite a comment for Mary to make."

"That was quiet a thing for Josephine to do," Benedict countered and looked at each man in their circular seating area. "What *do* we do now?"

"Nothing," Harlan said, and had his drink topped up

by the waiter. "We do nothing." He nodded at the young man before he hurried off to service another. "We don't worry. We follow the letter of the law in her home and we'll be fine."

"*You didn't*, filming and photographing her girls," Cyrus scorned.

Harlan grinned, his cigar between his teeth. "And I will continue to do so. But until Jo gives us a reason to worry, I won't be."

"Maybe we'd better find out then," Donald said. "And find out soon."

*****

Josephine entered her brownstone, locked both front doors behind her, and sighed. It has been a long morning and she'd only been out for three hours. She slowly wandered up to her room, undressed, and slid into a simple white dress and flats. Leaving the velvet dress hanging on her closet door, she put away her jewellery and hair accessories, and lay down for a few minutes, recalling the morning.

That scene in the church had been something. She had gone knowing she would do something, just didn't know what exactly. But after finding out there would be a procession past the coffin, she had made a beeline for it first. And the look on Mary's face… Oh, that bitch paled under her caked on make-up.

"She always did look like the clown from Stephen King's It," she muttered. "Don't know why she never bothered learning how to put it on properly." Another sigh came from her gut. "This business has become so damn tiring. And what was that stunt Cormac pulled? Just getting into my car when he felt like it and threatening me. Oh, I've got proof all right, and none of you want it to air or go public, but it will, believe me. But how the hell did it get this far? What made me say that in church? It's going to scare a lot of men, maybe put me out of business." She thought about that. "But am I really going to care if I go out of business. Didn't I say not long ago I need to retire. That seventy-five was the end. And then I got the feeling that I might not make seventy-five and goddamn it I go and threaten every man in church. Damn it!"

She rolled over and looked at her bedside clock. Two in the afternoon. She hadn't eaten since breakfast, and she had men coming in tonight. They hadn't cancelled at this point, because her clients were wide and varied, so many hadn't been there at the funeral.

She got to her feet and went downstairs for a bite to eat, and to prepare herself for later.

Chapter 6

Harlan spun around on the wheel in the sex room. "Whoo, I need to get me one of these. What do you call them?"

"An enfettered wheel." Josephine cracked the cat o' nine tails across Harlan's body as he spun around. "It's similar to a knife thrower's wheel. Except I'm not throwing knifes, I'm throwing my whip." Dressed in her Madam X leather outfit, Josephine cracked the whip left and right, leaving marks on Harlan's body. "You've never tried this before, why now?"

"Well…" He spun upside down. "I figured if shit was going to hit the fan thanks to Bartie, I better get in my first try. I like it. But I also wanted to talk to you."

"About?" The whip flew back and forth.

"What you said in the church at Bartie's funeral. Oh, I need to stop, I'm feeling sick."

Josephine pulled the wheel to a stop and set him upright. "Need a bucket? This isn't for everyone."

He was pale under the lighting. "I might. Get my hands undone, I need to sit down."

Josephine quickly untied his hands and legs and helped

him into a chair. She had a small kit near the door for those who became ill. A bucket, some first aid supplies, and smelling salts. She broke a capsule and shoved it under his nose. "Here, breathe in, it will set you straight."

He breathed in and coughed on the stench. "That's foul. What is it?"

"Ammonia." Josephine handed him the bucket. "Throw up in this. Now…" She grabbed another chair and placed it in front of him, seating herself as best she could in her clothing. "What's this about the shit hitting the fan?"

Harlan flashed a grin, even though his head was hanging over the bucket he was holding onto with both arms. "Everyone's worried about that little show you put on at the funeral. Telling the world you have evidence of our behaviour. I think it's hilarious, but others are worried."

"They have no need to be. If they leave my name out of what happened to Bartie, then I leave their names out of it. I just don't want to be blamed for his death when I had nothing to do with it."

"Fair enough. And considering what happens in my grotto, it's not like I have a right to complain about how you run things here." Harlan slowly breathed in and relaxed his grip on the bucket. "It's calmed now. I don't think I'm going to be sick."

"Just hang onto it for another few minutes. As I said, it's not for everyone. Back to the funeral. Cormac Ryan walked out with our mayor, and then made himself comfortable in the back of my car, threatening me to keep my mouth shut. I can't say I'm not worried about what could happen. I wish I had kept my mouth shut."

Harlan managed a chuckle. "No one wants their name out there. They must know if they do anything to you that a list will come out. Careers will be ruined if they open their mouths."

"I don't think they care." Josephine uncrossed her legs and sat straighter, her hands on her knees. She pondered a moment. "I think they thought my words were a threat, and again, I should have kept my mouth shut, but I'm not about to ruin my own life and career over men with fetishes. Just like my grandmother and mother before me, I have an uncanny knack for keeping everyone else's affairs private. They needn't worry. I won't be saying anything. If they do, on the other hand, then information will be leaked to newspapers and TV shows. They just need to keep their mouths shut."

Harlan studied her face. "How much longer do you think you'll be doing this, Jo?"

She sighed and collapsed on the outtake. "No idea, Harlan. But I've been thinking that seventy-five is a good round number to close out my business. Although..." Her mind wandered back to the thought of not making it to seventy-five.

"Although what?" he urged, putting down the bucket. "What?"

"It's nothing." She shook it off. "Maybe I'm just being silly. And maybe I'm just being old. I think this business has worn me out. So if it gets around, tell everyone to hang in for another three years and I'll be out of the business and they won't have to worry about me ever again."

"Just every other madam in New York," Harlan muttered and put his hand to his mouth in habit. He'd forgotten he couldn't smoke in the sex room and put his hand down.

"Yes, just every other madam. And that's a problem, isn't it?" she mused. "I'm not the only one. Not the only madam with girls. Prostitution is illegal, but they do nothing about it because they see the women running the brothels. If they shut it all down, they're left with nowhere to go, and it's all their fault. They made it illegal, but see the girls anyway, so they can hardly complain and shut it all down. The stories that would come out of that…" Her lips slid into a dirty smile and she get wearily got to her feet. "Ready to go again?"

"I am, but can we try something a little less…" He mentally searched for the right word. "Active."

She chuckled. "Of course, Harlan. It's your dime. I just dole out the punishment."

*****

Upstairs in the parlour, tongues were wagging.

"Should we even be here?"

"Why not? She's not telling."

"But she could, and then we'll all be outed."

"What are you so worried about?"

"This," he waved his hands around, "everything."

"Oh, for God's sake, Cyrus," Benedict complained. "Calm down. You always were a flighty one. We're all sitting here, waiting on our girls, as usual. Has anything happened? No. Has Jo let our secrets out? No. Just calm down or go home to your wife. *If* she's home, that is. Probably out banging her own man."

The others laughed, mocking Cyrus.

"Seriously, Cyrus," Bernard said. "She's scratching our back while we scratch hers. We'd be stupid to out her, especially if she has evidence of what's gone on here."

"Insurance." Howard nodded. "She knows what she's doing. As do we. We come here most nights, while our wives are waiting for us at home, and yet we have no problem doing it. We have no problem letting go of our struggles to keep our fetishes hidden. Here we can live and thrive and delight in them. She scratches ours, we scratch hers. And good for her if she has some sort of proof. I'd expect her to."

"Expect her to?" Cyrus stuttered. "She's taken what…" He glared around the room, looking for something. "Photos, videos, what? Are there hidden cameras in the rooms filming us? Is that even legal?"

"Well, Harlan said he'd taken photos, so what does it matter?" Bernard finished off his cognac. "Calm down, Cyrus. If we all keep our mouth shut we'll be fine."

"Oh, Bernie." Kaylin leant against the door frame and swung her right stocking clad leg forward while twirling a feather boa. "It's time for you to be punished in the blue room."

"Ooh." Bernard placed his empty glass on the coffee table in front of him and got to his feet. "Gentlemen, my time is up and I will see whoever's here when I leave." He made his way to Kaylin and linked arms as she led him upstairs.

"It's all well and good for him to say not to worry,"

Cyrus muttered. "We're both politicians. If we're outed, it will be the end of our careers."

"And if more judges and lawyers are outed it will be the end of theirs," Benedict pointed out. "We all have something to lose, Cyrus, not just politicians."

"I don't think we all do," Howard replied. "As a producer I may well get away with it. Donald as a director could get away with it. Harlan will most certainly get away with it. And any other people outside of law and politics will probably get away with it."

"Such as?" Cyrus asked before being interrupted by an interloper. "And you are?" He eyed the young man standing in the doorway. Twenty-something, he guessed, dark hair swept over to the side, ripped jeans and matching jacket with a ripped tank top underneath.

"Ah…" He dazedly stared at the men. "I'm ah here to see ma-madam."

"And you are?" Howard repeated, thinking he looked familiar.

"Ah…Romano Viera." The young man shoved his hands into his jeans pockets and became shy, tilting his head so his hair fell forward, shielding his eyes from them.

"Oh…" Howard nodded. "I know now. Some musician. I think my daughter was watching you on TV the other night and she suggested I put you in a movie. I see why she would say that. You're very good looking."

Romano, stage name Romeo, quickly perused the men in the parlour. He recognised none of them, but figured Howard must be some sort of director in order to say that. "Ah, that's nice of her. I ah…" He looked for a spare chair and found one in the corner near the curtain covered bay window. "I'll just stay here. Do we, ah, wait until we're called? Or something?" He wiped his sweaty palms on his jeans. They weren't the only part of him sweating. Everything was. This was the first time he'd been to see a madam and it had been on recommendation from a friend in the music industry. He'd called and booked in, having no idea what happened next.

"You wait until your girl is ready and she comes and gets you," Benedict told him. "Unless you're waiting on Madam X herself."

"Ah, no," Romano stuttered, embarrassed beyond belief. He still couldn't believe he was in a madam's brothel and he was about to do what he was about to do. The rigmarole just to get there was ridiculous. Driving into the garage, taking a staircase down to the undercover walkway and then let into the back door that led into the basement, then upstairs to the parlour.

"Benny, I'm ready for you," Allegra called from the doorway. "Come along, let me please you for the next hour."

"Well, that's me." Benedict stood up and smoothed his blazer. "Gentlemen, kid." He nodded to Romano. "Yours will turn up in a moment." He allowed Allegra to escort him downstairs.

Two more girls came for Howard and Cyrus, with a third coming for Romano five minutes later.

"Well, hello, big boy," Tallulah greeted him. She was dressed in a fuchsia corset with matching stockings, garter belt, and feather boa, which she draped around his neck. "First time here? I haven't seen you before." She slithered her ass over his lap and rubbed herself against him. "Let's get you going, huh. We have the rose room upstairs and I'll have you hard in no time." She swung around and pulled him to his feet. "How old are you? You look so young. Should you even be here?" A giggle slipped out. "You'd better be legal, considering this isn't. You do know that, right? That this job isn't legal? Did you come in the right way?" She pulled him over to the stairs and started up. "Don't worry, I'll make you come in no time."

*****

Josephine set her whip on its stand and sighed. "So what did you think?"

Harlan pulled on his smoking jacket. "Well, I gotta say, Jo, that's the best spanking I've ever had and I haven't had many in my life." He tied the belt and sighed. "It'd be a shame if some asshole shut you down because of Bartie. Stupid old bastard. Now we could all lose out because of him."

"Yes," she murmured. "It would be. Not that it matters much if I'm shutting up shop in the next couple of years. I'm seventy-two. Three more years until I'm seventy-five. I might go out with a bang."

She opened the door and waited for him to pass into the basement, then locked it behind him. "I do hope Allen and Cormac can keep it to themselves until we all retire. It would be more beneficial for them."

"And for us." Harlan nodded. "I'll see you in a couple of days, Jo. I might do this again sometime. It was… interesting."

She flashed a small smile and unlocked the basement door. "Harlan. See you next time." She watched him head down the underground walkway to the garage and locked the door. How many more nights of this she could take, she didn't know.

*****

The news of her behaviour at Bartie's funeral did nothing to dissuade men from coming to her establishment six nights a week. She still saw the politicians, lawyers, judges and officers. Still saw the musicians, singers, actors, directors and producers.

But it came as quite a surprise when Mary Winthrop turned up on her doorstep one day, knocking on her front door for the world to see.

Josephine collected herself and answered the door. "Mary, this is a surprise. What do you want?"

"To talk to you, *Ms* Pompadour." Mary stood steadfast, even though she was a good three inches shorter than Josephine.

"About?" Josephine sighed and crossed her arms. "I really don't care to discuss Bartie. Or you."

Mary pushed her way past and inside, pulling off her gloves. "Well, I want to."

Surprised, Josephine closed both doors and followed her into the sunny parlour. "And why's that? Because you want to know about your husband's exploits? Or because you want to know if there's someone else he may have left his money to?" She couldn't read Mary's face, so had no idea why she was there. "Just be careful with what you say, I'm prone to slapping."

Mary blanched. "I want to know why Bartie was coming here and for how long?"

"Didn't your detective tell you that?" Josephine sat in the easy chair by the bay window and calmly crossed her legs, smoothing her teal green woollen dress over her knees. "He should have."

Mary pursed her lips and slowly breathed in. It rankled her, having to be in this house with this woman.

Josephine noted the woman's expression. "Why are you actually here, Mary? You clearly don't want to be."

Mary took a step towards her. "How long did Bartie come here?"

"Bartie's been coming here for five years. But then, you know that." Josephine clasped her hands on her lap.

Mary moved another step. "And were you the only one he saw?"

A bemused smile slid across Josephine's lips. "No. But then you should *also* know that."

"Did he have a favourite?"

"He did."

"Did she have any diseases she may have passed on?"

"No. Did *he?*"

Mary reeled back. "Of course he didn't. How dare you say that?"

"Then why are you asking?" Josephine stormed to her feet. "What's the real issue here, Mary? The fact that Bartholomew fucked whores and got his ass whipped by a madam, or the fact he's left you out of his will…" Her eyes grew wide. "Is that it? He left you out of the will. Did he put me or my girls in his will?"

"Of course not, don't be absurd," Mary cried. "It doesn't matter what his will said, we were still married, I'll get everything, especially if he expected his sins to be hidden after his death."

"His sins?" Josephine cut in. "How gauche."

"Just like you," Mary barked. "You always thought you were better than you were, Josephine *Pompass*. I remember you from way back, in society. No one knew whose daughter you were. You didn't even like admitting to it back then and certainly didn't partake until your slut of a mother passed." Her head spun to the right and her hand flew to her left cheek.

Josephine lowered her hand. "If you call me that again, I will slap you again. Hell, you'll be lucky if I don't take a whip to your ugly-ass face. Now, why you're here, Mary, I have no idea. Whatever Bartie got up to while you were sunning your days away in California is up to him. I do know what he did here and in his sex crazed state ended up killing two of my girls. So don't take the high road with me, because that is something I will have no problem giving to the Press, or singing loud and clear from the rooftops. That Bartholomew Winthrop was a murderer. He killed two of the girls he was fucking and ended up killing himself while inside one."

Mary stumbled back in shock. "No, no, my Bartie wouldn't."

"*Your* Bartie," Josephine said scathingly. "Was a murdering old cunt who loved to get his dick sucked and his ass whipped. How is *that* going to sound on TV? Go home, Mary. Go home to California and take whatever he left you and leave me in peace. Because the faster you do that, the faster I keep my mouth shut and not reveal all about your filthy cunt of a husband." She walked menacingly towards her, making her back up to the door. "Go home, and tell your lawyer to wrap up the estate as quickly as possible. And if he did leave anything to someone besides you, then let it go. It's not like you're not rich in your own right. Unless you've blown that company stock money in your old age. But then, selling your New York houses should bring a pretty penny into the coffers." She opened the vestibule door. "Get out, Mary and leave me the fuck alone." She pulled open the front door and waved her out.

Mary hurried past and down to her limo parked at the curb. She turned back before she got in. "You'll pay for this, Josephine Pompadour."

"And if I do, so will every other person who's come here. Be prepared for that hell to be unleashed on you, Mary, because I will tell them it was all your fault." Josephine slammed and locked the door and did the same to the house door. "Miserable fucking bitch." She walked into the parlour and took her seat, watching the limo roll away. "Miserable fucking bitch," she repeated with less gusto and heaved a sigh from the pit of her gut. "Miserable…bitch. I can only hope she does exactly what I told her and go back to California."

*****

Mary's car parked in the driveway of her Hampton's home. Hidden by trees, and away from the road, she waited until he arrived and slid into the backseat beside her.

"Mary."

"Mr Mayor, so glad you could see me."

"Call me Allen," he replied smoothly. "Although, spending an hour just to come out here to talk to you in secret seems a bit much. Was it really necessary? Could we have not talked on the phone?"

"As I said on the phone, this is of the utmost importance." Her hands gripped one another in her lap. "It's about Bartie's…*after dark* activities. That dreadful woman turned up to his funeral and embarrassed me beyond belief. I cannot believe she did that. How could she?"

Allen breathed in. Josephine Pompadour was not a topic he wanted to discuss with Mary Winthrop. Or any wife for that matter. "There's not much I can do about that now, Bartie's gone and buried, and the funeral's over."

"But that woman is still allowed to run her brothel. How, Allen? Prostitution is illegal here in New York."

Allen apprised her. "What's really going on, Mary? Is it the fact Bartie saw a madam, or the fact you couldn't provide what she could? Or, is it something else that's going on?"

Shocked, Mary sent a scathing glare his way. "How *dare* you, Allen Gerard. You're the mayor of New York, you're supposed to be the one running this state."

"I run the city, not the state," he remarked dryly. "And what is it you expect me to do?"

"Stop her!" Mary demanded. "Embarrass her the way she embarrassed me at the funeral. Embarrass her for all to see."

"And do you realise how many men in power, including many who knew your husband well, would hate you for that?" Allen straightened his tie. "I will not put the livelihoods of thousands of men at risk for your vendetta, Mary Winthrop. And don't even think of blackmailing me, because that won't work. Your husband saw a madam and killed two of her girls. That was covered up for the privacy and protection of all involved, *including* your husband. If you want that information to come out, then go right ahead. I bet Jo will have great evidence of that. And *then* what will you think of your husband. *Then* what will *everyone else* think of your husband? The *murdering* judge."

"How dare you," Mary growled. "I thought, as the mayor of New York, that you, of all people, would do something to stop that Russian slut in her tracks. Clearly I was wrong."

"Is that why she slapped you in the church?" Allen huffed. "Called her a Russian slut? Is that it? From your attitude here today, I can see why you deserved it. Can it, Mary, I'm not going to do anything that will jeopardise thousands of people just because you want revenge. Get angry at Bartie. Hell, get angry at yourself for not being a good wife who couldn't do her duty. But don't get angry at me because I won't bow at your beck and call. That's not what I do, so screw you, *Mrs* Bartholomew Winthrop. Your husband was an ass, and so are you." Allen flung open the back door and stepped out, spinning around to say one more thing. "And don't even think of contacting me again. I won't be helping you, but God help you if you do harm to any of us. Be warned, Mary." He slammed the door and stalked over to his car. He was gone ten seconds later.

She sat huffing in the back seat, dabbing at her face as angry tears fell. If he wasn't going to do anything to seek revenge on behalf of Bartie, then she would.

*****

Allen fumed all the way back to the city, and as he crossed over to the island of New York, he called Josephine.

"Allen. Why are you calling?"

"Josephine. A warning. Mary Winthrop just called me to her Hampton's house to ask me to destroy you. I warned her that I wouldn't because the careers of thousands of men were at stake and to not do anything rash. I don't think she's going to heed my warning."

Josephine thought for a few moments. "It's okay. I can deal with the likes of Mary Winthrop. I have proof Bartie killed those girls. If she tries, she dies of embarrassment."

"Even though I can't do much, if shit goes down, Jo, we're not going down with you."

"Oh, Allen, but you will," Josephine told him. "You *all* will. At some point." She dropped the phone into its cradle and stared out the window. A cold suffocating feeling was holding on tight in her gut. She didn't have much longer.

*****

Over the next two weeks, Josephine spoke directly to every man who came through her back door. Would they support her if something were to happen? Would they run with their tale between their legs? Would they turn like a cut snake to save their own skin?

Of course they would support her.

Of course they wouldn't say anything.

They all lied.

She knew they were lying, that's what men did. So she gathered her evidence every day and kept it safe. She wrote letters to those she needed to write them to, and made countless phone calls. She gathered her money, stocks, and bonds into her safe, and spoke to her lawyer, making plans for what could be the inevitable. She knew something was coming. Something was going to happen. She just couldn't put her finger on it, but knew Mary Winthrop was going to make trouble for her.

She'd known that one day, the shit could hit the fan, and so over the years had switched out her heirlooms for replicas, and had paste imitations of her jewellery made. All of the real items were in storage.

She couldn't rely on the word of the johns coming to her establishment. They were going to bail at the first sign of trouble. She needed people she could rely on and gathered her army, making phone calls and obtaining confirmation that help would be there.

Now, it was just a matter of when.

*****

Josephine was in her back garden tending to the rose bushes. She had rows of them around the yard, and they provided her rooms with sweet smelling colour to help combat the odour many men left behind. Thank God for windows and air freshener.

She came to the last two she had planted, just stalks at this point as they had only been planted a couple of months ago. One for Harmony, and one for Heaven.

A rose bush each so she could remember them and how they had lost their lives on her property. Something she deeply regretted.

She had been watching the cameras when that Carmelo boy had attacked Kaylin, but not when Bartie had been with either girl. If only she had been, she could have reached them faster. But she hadn't and she didn't.

Josephine gave the bushes a water and got to her feet. She was worn out, just from doing some gardening on a Sunday morning. But she had the remainder of the day to rest and Hilda was cooking a delicious roast meal for lunch.

Wiping her brow, she gathered her things and walked down to the basement where she left the gardening tools in the small storage room next to the laundry. She locked the back door and walked upstairs, hearing the front door bell ring out.

Chapter 7

"Josephine Pompadour, I am placing you under arrest for solicitation and prostitution. Anything you can and do say will be held against you in a court of law." Cormac Ryan shoved the arrest warrant into Josephine's chest and strode past her stunned face, through the vestibule, and into the hallway of her brownstone. "Search everywhere. Search everything. Pull it apart if you have to."

Josephine watched his imposing figure stand in her home and saw her housekeeper scurry from the back hallway into the kitchen. She didn't need to tell her staff to call her lawyer in times of need. Such as being arrested. They knew to automatically do it without being told.

"And why now after all this time, Cormac?" she asked, but was pushed aside as officers filed past her. She walked into the house. "After everything that's happened. Why now? Why me?"

"You should know the answer to that," Connor Ryan told her as he waltzed through the door. "After everything you've done." He grabbed the banister and took the stairs two at a time while his younger brother Declan headed downstairs. Both were detectives in the NYPD.

"It's time." Cormac confronted her, and waved an officer over. "I'm placing you under arrest. Put out your hands."

The officer held up his cuffs and scored a hate-filled side-eye from Josephine. "Ma'am, your hands."

Reluctantly, she held them out in front of her. "Considering everything that's happened here, Cormac, you all might live to regret this."

"Oh, I doubt it." He stared her down. "There's not much you can do."

"Wouldn't be so sure of that," she replied and heard an almighty crash from the kitchen. "Hey! I'll make you pay for that."

"We have the right to search." Cormac walked into the front parlour. "Search the lot."

"You have the right to search, not break." Josephine's tone was scathing. "You break it, you pay for it. My items are expensive and some are priceless." She followed him into the front room and saw four officers going through the built-in wood shelves full of treasures from her yearly journeys. She watched one officer shove a crystal figurine off the shelf. Her gaze following it to the floor where it smashed into a thousand pieces. Ice froze her heart. It had been from her mother from their homeland of Russia and now it lay dead on the floor.

Josephine's furious burning gaze turned to Cormac. "You all have no problem coming to visit my girls, yet this is the way you betray me. By breaking my things that mean the world to me." Her voice lowered. "You will pay for this, Cormac Ryan. Your *entire family will pay.*"

Cormac coolly glanced at her. "I'd like to see you try anything. Tear this place apart." He walked off, leaving her with the officer guarding her.

Close to tears, but boiling inside, Josephine looked behind her to see the love seat near the window, a replica of a priceless piece from the Russian royal family. Unable to watch them tear her life apart she sat down with her back to them. Not once had this happened in her fifty plus years of being a madam. No officer, commissioner, or mayor had demanded her arrest, knowing full well they would be found out for attending her Upper East Side brownstone. Not one wanted their wives to know they were pleasured by hookers, prostitutes, whores. So they'd left her alone legally while being attended to illegally by her and her girls.

But this was something else.

Josephine watched as replica paintings were ripped from the dark mahogany wood walls, the couches were slashed open, all of her trinkets on the cupboards thrown to the floor and smashed. Her whole life was being ripped apart and there was nothing she could do about it.

Two officers tipped over cupboards while two more walked behind the love seat and yanked the rich blue velvet curtains from their rods.

"What did you expect to find in a pair of curtains?" she mocked, and was roughly pulled from the seat. "Do not manhandle a woman! Least of all an elderly one. What are you doing?" She watched the love seat be slashed open. "That's a royal artefact you stupid boy."

A crash came from down the hall and she ran out of the parlour before they could stop her. "What is going on?" She came to a halt in the kitchen doorway and saw her frightened maid and housekeeper cowering in the corner. "Hilda, Fanny, are you all right?"

A pile of plates was knocked to the floor and she winced at the sound, sending a scathing glare at the officer who looked back with a nonchalant shrug, she recognised him from his midnight visits. "But then you've been here enough to know where everything is. Since you do like to stop off in the kitchen for coffee before you leave."

The officer's face changed from white to red and his fellow officers stopped their battery of the kitchen long enough to look at him as he picked up another pile of plates and dropped them on the floor.

"Don't think your career will go anywhere after this. Especially when it comes out." She strode off down the hall to find Cormac standing at the top of the first floor stairs. "Are my staff under arrest as well or just I?"

Cormac gazed down at the seventy-two year old in her plain black dress. Her grey hair was piled into a neat bun, her skin still plump and youthful. "They're free. For now."

"Hilda, Fanny, come here, please," she called down the hall.

Her staff quickly hurried down the hall, clinging to each other as they made their way past the officers.

"Go next door and call Rocco. Let him know what's happening. He took Myrtle shopping. Tell them not to come back. I have no idea how long this will take."

They nodded and stepped over to the door, frightened to their cores. But two officers put up their hands to hold them back.

"They're not under arrest, so they're free to go," Josephine said coldly.

The officers looked up at the commissioner, who nodded, and they stepped aside for the two women. Josephine waited for them to leave before glaring up at Cormac. "How much longer?"

"Longer," he replied and walked away.

Officers with axes, crowbars, and chainsaws marched through the doorway.

"What now?" she demanded. "Are you seriously going to attack my furniture?"

"Not your furniture," Alec Ryan stated, stopping beside her and smoothing his light grey Italian silk suit. "The brownstone. Start in the parlour, boys. Rip it to shreds." He followed them into the room.

"Are you sure that's what you want to do?" she pressed on, watching the back of his head. "Considering."

Alec spun around, panic on his face. "Considering what?"

She remained steely. "Sonja."

"Sonja what?" He moved closer to her, his eyes boring into hers. "Sonja what?"

"Sonja decorated the entire interior of this house not ten years ago."

The panic subsided. "Well, yes, she did. But it's not like she's going to be upset."

"Isn't she?" Josephine murmured. "The attention this receives alone will upset many, many, members of high society in this city."

Alec's sapphire blue eyes narrowed. A trait from his father, Cormac, along with the wavy brown hair. "Is that a threat?"

"That's a promise," she stated and arched a brow in defiance.

*****

"What's this for?" an officer asked, lying on top of the rack.

"It's a stretching rack," another replied and quickly snapped a photo with his small camera that he'd hidden in a pocket.

"And this? What is it?" The officer spun around. "The Wheel of Fortune wheel?"

"That's a wheel where you tie a person to it and throw knives at them as they spin around," a fourth officer told them. "They use them in circuses."

The second officer took more photos as the others tried out the equipment. They had been searching the rooms in the basement when they had come across a locked door and broken it down, finding all sorts of weird contraptions along with whips, blindfolds, and other BDSM items.

"What do we have here?" Declan paused in the doorway. "A sex room. Naughty, naughty, Madam X. I wonder how many asses got spanked in this room." He walked through the doorway and a chill sped down his spine.

"And how do you know, detective?" the officer taking photos asked.

"I saw some of this on a case last year," Declan replied smoothly. "And there've been rumours about a sex room for a few years." He looked at each piece and each officer. "We're going to have to take all of this."

"All of it?" An officer looked around. "How're we getting it out?"

"We have the movers coming in for everything we're taking. They'll be here in," he checked his watch, "about fifteen minutes."

Connor came bouncing into the room. "Whoa, what do we have here?" He excitedly looked around, hands on hips, grin on lips. "Awesome!"

Declan rolled his eyes. "Glad you think so. But this place is making me sick."

"Not like you haven't been in a sex room before," Connor joked, slapping his brother on the shoulder as he passed. "You would know some of those machines intimately."

"What are you insinuating?" Declan wheeled on his older brother, sapphire eyes boring into sapphire eyes. They both had the same wavy brown hair cut into the same short back and sided regulatory style. And even though they were two years apart, they looked nothing alike except for those two features.

"Come on, Declan," Connor snapped, stepping closer so their noses touched. "I know your predilections for sex, so don't pretend to be a choir boy."

"Boys." Cormac stopped at the bottom of the stairs. "You finished down here?"

Declan moved away from his brother. "Yeah. We've searched the rooms, found the sex room, and now we're just waiting on the removalists."

"Ah, sir, Ms Pompadour ran upstairs to her bedroom. Do we let her go?" An officer stopped halfway down the stairs and leant over the railing.

"That's fine, follow her," Cormac said. Once the officer went upstairs, he let out a deep sigh. "I hope this doesn't turn out to be a nightmare."

Alec walked down the stairs and caught his father's comment. "Why would it?" He stood beside him. The three eldest Ryan boys, a lawyer and two detectives, all looked like their father in one way or another. "She won't say anything."

"We can't be sure, which is why we need to find what she has. Pop says she'll have the proof somewhere in the house."

"But do we know that for a fact?" Alec asked.

Another sigh before Cormac spoke. "I don't know."

*****

Josephine watched the officers trash her bedroom on the top floor of the brownstone.

Filled with dark wooden furniture, it could be suffocating with so little space, but she loved the cosiness of it. The four poster bed took up a large portion of the room, with two tall chests of drawers on the wall beside it, and the large wardrobe on the wall opposite.

Her clothes had been strewn across the floor; the bedding flung across them. All of the furniture had belonged to her mother and grandmother, but the fear of this very day happening had driven her to put them all in storage and find replicas. Her chests held the china jug and matching basin of her grandmother, and the china teapot and cup and saucer set of her mother. They were her most personal possessions, except for the glass figurines and travel knick-knacks downstairs. Her mother and grandmother used the bed for sleeping, the desk for writing, and it had all been handed down.

She watched in horror as the teapot and cup smashed to the floor into thousands of pieces and then opened her mouth. "You stupid fucking bastard. That was an heirloom from my mother," she screeched. "How fucking dare you trash my house when all you had was a search warrant. It's not a smash and trash warrant. They were heirlooms."

The officer, while taken aback at her screeching and language, didn't care and proceeded to send the jug and basin the same way as the china.

Josephine flew into a rage, attacking the officer with her hands. Clawing at his eyes, ears and nose. "I hate you, you filthy fucking pig. I hate you."

Two other officers pulled her off as Cormac entered the room. "What's going on?"

"You bastard," Josephine panted, tendrils of hair falling out of her bun. "You bastard pigs are smashing heirlooms and not giving a damn. Even though half of them have been here to see my girls. Just like your sons. Just like you—"

Cormac's hand flew over her face. The crack loud enough to be heard around the room.

"That's enough," a commanding voice said from the doorway. "You've far overstepped your mark, Commissioner."

"Oh, Carlyle," Josephine gasped, sagging to the floor. "They're trashing my house. They're trashing my belongings. Prized heirlooms just…gone." She picked up a piece of china from the pot. "My mother's…"

"Seriously, Commissioner." Carlyle Houston, Josephine's

lawyer of thirty years, walked over to his client. "You should be ashamed of yourself, but you're probably not. Like all of the Ryan men. Arrogant to the core." He helped Josephine to her feet. "Where's the search warrant?"

An officer picked it up and Carlyle quickly read through it. "As I thought. Nothing about trashing my client's belongings. You will be paying for this, Cormac. Mark my words. I'm taking my client downstairs. I saw the mess of that when I arrived."

Cormac remained silent. He knew he had overstepped, but had been told to go hard by his bosses. What was done was done.

Carlyle led his client downstairs, but stopped on the first floor. They watched as walls and floors were ripped apart in bedrooms used by clients.

"What are they doing," she cried, her hands balling up and moving to her mouth in shock. "My house. My beautiful house."

"Unfortunately, in this city, the cops think they can do what they like." Carlyle continued down to the parlour. "Good grief!"

Every piece of furniture had been slashed, tipped over, or pulled apart. He righted the love seat and sat her on it. "This is despicable. On Sunday of all days."

She managed to find the strength to huff. "Of course it's on a Sunday. The only day we have off because they need to go to church with their wives to repent for their sins." An idea came to mind. "But where will they all go now they've raided and ransacked my house? No other madam in New York has a sex room. And I'm not too sure many will remain open now I've been raided."

Carlyle watched the holes in the walls grow bigger and despaired for his client. "Neither do I. They've shot themselves in the foot."

"Both feet," Josephine uttered in anger, her eyes tearing up at the destruction. The only home she'd known for the last seventy-two years was being pulled from her grasp with every swing of the axe. "What do I do, Carlyle?"

Her lawyer sighed and slid his hands into his pants pockets. "I don't think there's much you can do. Your clients did this. Shot themselves in the ass by taking away the one place they come to outside of their marriage. They won't stop this. They started this. They're the ones who set this up. They're the ones who want to take you down."

"There's only one way I can take them down first," Josephine muttered. "Release the proof."

"And where is it?" Carlyle watched his client's face. She was depressed and dejected, but a determination glinted in her eyes.

"Safe."

Cormac came down the stairs and saw the removal teams coming in the door. "Down in the basement, boys. We want all of it."

Declan and Connor came up the stairs and directed them down.

"We all done?" Declan glanced into the parlour. "That her lawyer?"

"It is." Cormac's thick brows furrowed and Carlyle's gaze turned to his.

"Do we have something to worry about?" Declan noticed the lawyer's angry expression. "He's pissed and she's his top client."

"Is she?" Connor gazed at the lawyer. "Surely he has other clients beside her."

"Oh, he does," Cormac replied. "High profile, powerful clients who may or may not have used her services."

Connor gave a low whistle. "They won't be happy. We done here? It's Sunday and are we still having family lunch."

"We'll have dinner instead." Cormac briefly smiled. "Seven p.m., don't be late. The two of you can go. Declan, go be with your wife and son, Connor, go be with your son."

"I think he's at the house anyway with his cousins." Connor slapped his old man's back. "See you at home. Declan?"

"Yeah." Declan gave a last glance at Josephine Pompadour. New York City's top madam, and walked out the door. "See you at home."

Cormac watched his two middle sons leave and stepped over to the parlour to allow the removalists to get the sex room contraptions out of the house. He knew there was something he was missing.

"Have Declan and Connor left yet?" Alec asked, taking the last few steps down to the ground floor. "We're going through everything upstairs and it's all been recorded."

"They have. You should, too. Sonja and the kids will be waiting for you. We're having dinner instead of lunch."

"Okay. I'll see you at home later." Alec looked into the parlour. "There's going to be a lot of scared men in New York tonight."

"Yeah." Cormac frowned. "Too many men in power who can ruin careers."

"I'll see you later." Alec slapped his back and left.

Cormac's gaze hadn't left Josephine the whole time, and all he saw was a frightened, but determined old woman. How the hell one woman could have so much power over men was astounding. But then, when they had their pants down around their feet, everyone was vulnerable to being controlled.

He stepped aside for his officers when they were done tearing the parlour apart.

"Didn't find anything, sir," one said. "You need us anywhere else?"

"Go ask the others if they need help," Cormac replied. "We should be nearly done." He waited until they were alone before walking into the parlour. The walls had been torn apart, the floor pulled up.

"An absolute fucking mess," Josephine muttered. "You're daughter-in-law's really going to love knowing you tore her work to pieces."

"That's right, Sonja did a remodel for you. She did a good job." Cormac gazed around. "But you won't have the opportunity to hire anyone to fix all of this up."

"I'll have my client out tomorrow," Carlyle informed him.

"Will you?" Cormac asked. "Will you really, Carlyle? Prostitution is illegal in New York."

"And you're yet to arrest any other madam or prostitute," Carlyle snapped. "Or did you want my client to be the first you arrested? Make a show of it, a point. This is what will happen to the rest of you if you don't stop servicing them men of New York. Tell me, Cormac, how many powerful men do you know come here to my client's house? How many will have to recuse themselves from this case? How many will get caught up in the scandal you have now brought upon them? Upon the city. The congressmen, the judges, lawyers, TV and radio personalities? How many people are going to thank you for what you've done?"

"It was some of those people who demanded this." Cormac looked from him to Josephine. "You're done, Madam X. The men of this city are sick and tired of you getting away with this."

"And I was sick and tired of Bartie Winthrop killing my girls." Josephine surged to her feet. "I'm glad he's dead of a heart attack. That old bastard deserved it and the rest of you better be warned. I have proof and you won't find it, but I will have it released if I'm not." Her steely gaze defied his. "And don't think you're off the hook, Cormac. None of your family is."

"Did you get her?"

All three looked to the doorway to see Douglass Ryan. Ex PC of the NYPD, and Cormac's father, standing in the hallway.

"Yeah, Pop. We got her. And we're searching the house now. Should be finished soon."

"Good." Douglas stared at Josephine. "It's about time. Pity it had to be Sunday."

"The only time you're all not here being serviced by my girls," Josephine retorted. "You all go to church to repent for your sins and we get a rest." Her brow arched. "Including you and your catholic leanings."

Douglas shifted uncomfortably. "Good to see you're in cuffs. Should have been behind her back," Douglas replied.

"Why?" Carlyle asked. "So they could rip her clothes off and abuse her, like your son did when he slapped her. The power you two think you have…" He shook his head in disgust. "You're both pathetic."

"I want to speak to Josephine," Douglas stated. "Alone."

"So you can attack my client?" Carlyle scoffed. "No."

"It's okay," Josephine told him. "Step into the hallway while Douglas and I chat."

"You sure?" Carlyle gently touched her elbow.

"Yes. Just watch, don't listen." Her gaze darted to the PC. "You too, Cormac."

The two men nodded and made their way into the hall. Able to see, but not hear.

Douglas stepped closer to Josephine and kept his voice low. "Where is it?"

Her eyes narrowed. "Where's what?"

"You know damn well what I'm talking about. The list," he said furtively. "Where is it?"

"What list?" she mocked. "My shopping list?"

He ground his jaw and growled. "The list of men in your service. I know you have one. I've heard the rumours."

"Rumours? Unless you've heard it yourself out of my mouth, you shouldn't believe rumours. Rumours from whom? Who claimed it?"

"Just tell me where it is and this will all be over," Douglas said.

Josephine laughed. "You have got to be kidding me? Admit to something I don't have so you will do something you don't mean? Good God, Douglas. You just want to cover your own ass and those of your family and friends. There *is* no list." She walked over to Carlyle and Cormac. "Since this charade has gone on long enough, let's get it over with. I cannot *wait* to release all of my proof to the world. I'll be out tomorrow."

"I don't think so," Cormac said as the ripping of wood sounded out from above. "It's the end for you, Josephine Pompadour."

"We'll see," she replied confidently. "In the meantime, I'll have my lawyer sue you and the city for destruction of property. Someone has to fix all of this mess. I'll get Sonja in again, shall I? She was so good last time."

"We're done here." Cormac waved forward two officers standing in the doorway. "Take Ms Pompadour to the station and charge her."

Josephine's face turned into a scowl. "And I'll see you in court."

Chapter 8

"I cannot believe I was held overnight. In prison of all places," Josephine complained to her lawyer the next morning. "Why was I kept in there all night, Carlyle? Why couldn't you get me out?"

"Because it was Sunday, which is why I think you were arrested yesterday. So you couldn't get out even though I filed an emergency injunction." Carlyle paced back and forth in front of her in the courthouse hallway. "I called every judge, the district attorney, none of them wanted to know about the case until today. I think they're scared to touch it."

"They'd better be. Many of them frequented by abode." Josephine carefully pushed back her hair. She had not changed from her Sunday dress. Hadn't been able to shower or clean up. Just hauled out of her cell and dragged to the courthouse, and in desperate need of freshening up. "And why in God's name am I still in handcuffs?"

Carlyle stared pointedly at the officer standing beside his client. "Uncuff her. She hasn't killed anyone."

"No can do, sir." He shook his head. "We were told not to."

"By whom?" Carlyle asked. "There is no law that says someone on charges of this nature needs to be handcuffed. Has she caused a fight? Tried to run? No. Uncuff her."

The officer calmly stared him down. "No."

Carlyle gritted his teeth and seethed. "This case is really pissing me off now. Jo, you ready to use what you have."

"If I'm not released today, hell yes," she replied as the door to the courtroom swung open.

"Pompadour."

"That's us." Carlyle helped Josephine to her feet. "Let's hope we have a judge who's willing to be lenient and let you out."

Josephine rolled her eyes and let him lead her into the room and they stood behind the desk, waiting for their emergency hearing to start.

A judge walked into the room and up to his desk, while the district attorney took his place behind the desk opposite Carlyle's.

Josephine whispered in Carlyle's ear. "Eugene Haskell and Everett Lloyd have been to see me."

Carlyle kept his gaze on the judge, but nodded.

The judge banged his gavel. "We are now in session for an emergency hearing for Ms," he put his glasses on and squinted at the paperwork in front of him, "Ms Josephine…" His face paled and his gaze darted up to the defendant.

"Hello, Eugie," Josephine called, a secretive smile on her lips as she waved her fingers at him.

Judge Haskell stared at her, knowing full well where this was going next.

"Your honour, the district attorney's office is demanding that Josephine Pompadour stay behind bars." Everett stared at the judge. "Your honour? Are you okay?"

"No, he's not," Carlyle muttered before calling out, "Judge Haskell, I demand the release of my client. She's not a murderer, and not accused of murdering anyone, in fact the case against her is weak at most. I demand the release of my client."

Eugene didn't speak, his mouth was hanging open and he was staring at Josephine.

Josephine was staring back, wondering whether he was going to have her released from custody.

Everett glanced between the two. "Your honour? Is there something you need to tell the court? Your honour?"

"My client has been arrested for no good reason, your honour," Carlyle continued. Knowing he could lose control of the situation if Everett made the judge recuse himself. "I want her released, and after that shockingly horrid display the police department put on in her house yesterday, I will be suing them on behalf of my client. She doesn't have a habitable abode thanks to them, and will now have to stay in a hotel while it's fixed."

"The brownstone, and all of its…" Everett blushed. "*Furnishings,* has been taken into custody by the state of New York. It's evidence in her case."

"*You* took the evidence," Carlyle glared at his opponent. "You took equipment from the basement and trashed the rest of the house. You don't get to take custody of a person's home after slashing it to shreds and trashing her personal belongings, like the antiques handed down from her grandmother and mother."

"It was all part of the raid and the NYPD were well within their rights to take what they wanted," Everett argued.

"But not to trash her property or slap her across the face which Cormac Ryan did." Carlyle spun around and glared at the commissioner who was slinking down in his seat at the back of the courtroom. "Oh, yes you did, Commissioner. And I will be suing you for assault on my client's behalf, and filing a complaint with every agency that deals with police corruption." He turned back to the judge. "This can be over with her release. My client should never have been arrested and the charges are dodgy. Prostitution, for God's sake? A *seventy-two year old woman* is accused of being a madam and running a brothel. Do you *even know* what she does in her house, Judge?" He glared pointedly at Haskell who paled further. "Judge Haskell? I demand my client's release."

"And I demand that she be held in maximum security," Everett argued.

"You what!" Carlyle demanded. "Are you fucking crazy? Maximum security for what? Entertaining friends by having parties?"

"Order, order." Eugene banged his gavel. "There will be no use of profanities in this courtroom. Besides, I've made my decision. Ms Josephine Pompadour, you are to be remanded in court until your trial, for which a date will be set—"

"Then I suggest you recuse yourself, Judge Haskell," Carlyle demanded, glancing from a shocked Josephine to a scared Eugene. "If you don't release my client right now and drop all charges, then we will be forced to release information we know. The same for you, *District Attorney*." Carlyle turned to Everett. "You need to recuse yourself, as well. If the charges are not dropped right now, then I will make it so we get a new judge and lawyer for this case."

Everett huffed. "And what information could you have in order for me to recuse myself?"

Carlyle stepped back so Everett could see Josephine.

She wiggled her fingers at him and smiled. "Everett."

Carlyle stepped back and watched Everett's face pale to the same shade of white at the judge's. "You both need to drop these charges now. Or our information will be made public."

Everett swallowed the lump in his throat. "I have no idea what you're talking about," he stuttered and slumped into his seat. "No idea." His gaze darted to Eugene.

Carlyle followed his gaze and stared at the judge. "Judge Haskell. Release my client now."

Eugene stared back, his heart pounding in his chest. Fear making double time. *What information does he have?* he asked himself. *Could he know that I've seen Jo's girls on several occasions? Could she have told him? Considering the smirk on her face, I'd say she has. But can she prove it? Well, there are cameras now that can take undercover footage. But would she have done that to us? Would she risk it? She wouldn't. But she could. And what if she has something?*

He breathed in to quell his raging heart and fear. "I'm sorry, Mr Houston, I am not releasing your client."

"On whose orders are you to keep her in jail?" Carlyle asked.

"What?" Eugene shook his head. "What do you mean? I'm not taking orders, I'm remanding her to detention."

"You sure about that, judge? Considering the charges, and what you're claiming she does. If she is what the documents say she is, imagine *all* of the careers and reputations being put at risk by your actions. They aren't going to appreciate this, Eugene."

Everett kept his mouth shut. How could he prosecute a person he'd been to see. He was just as guilty as she. She gave, he partook. As did dozens of others, many he knew personally, and saw there often.

He rallied. "I know nothing about that, Mr Houston. These are serious charges, and the NYPD would not have raided her house without good authority."

"Sure. Good authority from higher-ups. I see it was your signature on the warrant. And since when does the commissioner of the NYPD personally raid people's houses and slap homeowners?"

Eugene blanched and the red rash quickly expanded up his neck to his face. "I know nothing of that. You will have to bring it up during the trial."

"There won't be a trial if you release my client with no charge," Carlyle pushed. "Judge."

Haskell fretted and scratched at the rash on his left hand. It had flared up twenty-four hours ago when pressured by the mayor and politicians to sign the arrest warrant and keep her in jail. "I've made my decision, Mr Houston. Your client is to be remanded in jail."

"Then you leave me with no choice, your honour. But I do suggest that my client is allowed a change of clothes and a shower, like other prisoners." Carlyle gently squeezed Josephine's shoulder. They had lost. For now. "And that yourself and the district attorney recuse yourselves for us to start fresh this week when the trial starts."

"The trial won't be starting this week," Eugene replied.

"I don't know when—"

"It will!" Carlyle said. "After tomorrow." He picked up his briefcase and walked out after Josephine was led back to the hallway. "Don't worry. Tomorrow will be a different day. We'll get them. Meanwhile, I'll come with you to the remand centre and make sure you're treated well."

"Thank you, Carlyle. I was so sure he'd let me go." Josephine sighed. "So sure." She looked down at her dirty dress and flats. "I tried to clean it…" she muttered.

"Once you're settled with a change of clothes, I'll get someone to get you some things. I'll also get the house back and pack up your property, putting it in storage. Then I'll leave and deal with our little problem. This is going to be fun."

"For you." Her expression was full of sorrow and mistrust. "But not for me."

*****

The next morning, all of the papers showed judge Eugene Haskell and district attorney Everett Lloyd in compromising positions in bed with women who were not their wives.

When Eugene sat down with his wife in their Upper East Side fifteenth floor penthouse apartment to eat his breakfast of one boiled egg, one slice of dry toast, and one black coffee, no sugar, he picked up the newspaper, shook it open, saw the images, and promptly had a heart attack.

He died moments later, his butler unable to revive him. His wife unable to look at his dead face after seeing how happy it was with a woman on his dick.

When Everett walked into his dining room, his wife threw the paper at him, and then another, and another.

"How dare you!" she screeched in her shrill voice. "How dare you disrespect me so publicly. Get out of this house and don't come back?"

Everett tried to explain as crockery flew at his head. "Honey, I have no idea what's going on. It's not true." He ducked and missed a plate to his head, but when he stood up he copped a cup in the eye. "Ow. Stop it, Vera. It isn't true. Nothing about this story is true. It's all lies."

"Oh, sure, Everett. It's not like you haven't cheated before. I know full well about that slut in Jersey." She threw cutlery at him. "Get out of this house. I'm taking you for everything you have, you motherfucking cheating whore."

Everett ran from the room, taking refuge in his office. He called Eugene's residence, but got the butler. He was too late and made his condolences. He then called the mayor and was told to deal with it.

Oh, he was going to deal with it, all right.

So was the mayor, and every other person who'd gone to see Madam X.

*****

Carlyle had filed another emergency hearing and they were back in another courtroom that afternoon.

"Your honour. I want my client released on her own recognisance. It has yet to be proven that she has done anything wrong. We have the judge dropping dead from a heart attack, the district attorney withdrawing from the case. Both have been replaced with yourself and Ms Pérez. My client is yet to be charged with anything. Her home has been confiscated for no reason."

"It's a crime scene, Mr Houston," Judge Isadora Crawford replied, reading through the paperwork. "But I can see that you're right, to a degree. She hasn't been charged yet, which is strange. But her house is a crime scene."

"No one died, your honour. Why's it a crime scene?" Carlyle asked. His light grey shiny suit reflected the lights of the courtroom and stood out for the photographers that had been allowed to attend.

Josephine had a clean blue knit dress on with matching flats. Her hair braided to one side.

"While you are correct, Mr Houston, the arrest warrant is for prostitution in the state of New York. I'm going to assume her residence is where the acts took place." Crawford looked from Carlyle to Josephine. "While it would seem that Judge Haskell and District Attorney Lloyd may have visited your establishment—"

"Who said it was my client's establishment where they were enjoying their tête-à-têtes? It could have been the other women's bedrooms," Carlyle objected. "Where's the proof those photos have anything to do with my client?"

"The photos the police took match the description of the bedrooms they were both in," Crawford said. "From yesterday's hearing minutes you very clearly stated that you had information you would release. Are you telling me those photos were not taken in Ms Pompadour's house?"

"Technically they're not photos, and technically they

weren't taken," Carlyle said with a point of a finger. "I did suggest they recuse themselves. They did not."

"Are you now saying that it was you who spread your information on Judge Haskell and District Attorney Lloyd to the Press?"

"I did no such thing, your honour," Carlyle replied truthfully. "It was not me who spread that information."

"Semantics, Mr Houston. Look…" Crawford sighed and leaned back in her chair. "I fully understand this is going to be a very sticky trial moving forward. There will be men of all careers who do not wish for this information to get out. And, while there really is no reason for Ms Pompadour to remain in remand, I also don't see a need to release her. Release her to where? Her home has been confiscated, so unless you'd put her up in your home, I'm going to suggest she be remanded in the women's wing of Edgecombe Correctional Facility to keep her safe from those who may now wish her dead. She will not be given special privileges, but considering her age, and her career choice, lightweight detention is the go. She can receive visitors and make phone calls, plus have some things in her cell. I'll set the first trial date for…" Crawford looked at her calendar. "Next Monday. We'll try and get this over with as soon as possible, Ms Pompadour. Mr Houston, anything else you wish to say?"

Carlyle glanced down at a troubled Josephine. Her brows deeply furrowed, her hands grasped on the table in front of her. "Jo?"

She gazed up at him and shook her head. "I need to see someone."

"If you aren't going to release my client, judge, then

we will accept that. Ms Pompadour needs to see someone, and I need her house back to try and recover her smashed and trashed personal belongings."

"I'll allow for you and some packers to go in and take what you need. The house was thoroughly searched and photographed. There's no real need for them to keep a hold on it, but I won't release it just yet because of the trial. You can go in for your client, though, to get her belongings. Anything else?"

Carlyle glanced once more at Josephine who again shook her head. "No, your honour."

Crawford banged her gavel. "This hearing is over, take Ms Pompadour back into custody and make sure she is *carefully* and respectfully transported to Edgecombe until Monday. Next hearing."

Georgia Pérez stood and smooth her black blazer over her matching skirt. "The easiest hearing I've ever won," she said to Carlyle. "Didn't have to say a thing."

"Lucky you," he mocked and gave a curt nod. "Georgia."

Her thick red lined lips turned into a smirk. "Carlyle. No need to get annoyed that you didn't win."

Carlyle paused and turned back. "There was no winning here today, Georgia. This is wrong, on every level. I'll see you on Monday."

*****

That afternoon, Carlyle walked into Josephine's house with her staff, and a small crew of packers and movers. "Let's get to work. We don't have long. Whatever is broken, carefully wrap it up and take it. Take the furniture as is, antiques can be repaired. Pack up her clothes, linen, everything, regardless of being damaged. I want nothing left for the cops to pick through, nothing left for anyone else to come and demolish."

The staff got to work carefully wrapping up their mistresses broken items and clothing, plus their own that they hadn't been able to take on Friday. Furniture was carried out to the moving van, and Carlyle made good time checking each and every room for what he could find. He knew Jo had multiple safety deposit boxes full of evidence to use, but she refused to hand the key over and didn't have it in her possession when arrested. Which meant it was still here. It also wasn't him who leaked the information about Eugene and Everett. He'd made a phone call to someone, and then the papers got the information. So Josephine clearly had someone working in secret for her.

He searched her desk and wardrobe, looked under the bed. If it was going to be anywhere, it would have to be somewhere safe. Unless the staff had it.

He walked down to the hallway outside of Hilda's bedroom door which was next to Fanny and Myrtle's. "Ladies. Where did Josephine store the keys to her safety deposit boxes? Where did she store the personal items such as her ledgers, diaries, etc?"

Hilda paused her packing. "I cannot tell you, Mr Houston. Madam swore me to secrecy and I plan on taking that information to my grave." She closed the lid of her suitcase. "Where is everything going?"

"Into storage. She said she had a storage site somewhere in Jersey. I'm worried the cops will find it and raid it."

"Aye. If she wanted it to go there, I can deal with that. I know the one." Hilda set her case and bag in the doorway. "I keep a lot of my mistresses secrets, I don't intend to start blabbing them now. But she did say that in the case of something happening, we would be taken care of."

Carlyle nodded. "She told me to make sure your wages still went into your accounts. I'm not sure if they can, considering they froze her bank accounts and assets, but I'll see to it that's reversed come Monday when the trial starts. It's not fair to her staff and everyone who relied on her that they should go without. In the meantime, I need to know everything else she's got."

Hilda shook her head. "Not unless she tells me herself to tell you. Can I get in to see her?"

"You can, she's allowed visitors." He glanced at Fanny and Myrtle. "Do you ladies have everything? All of your belongings, Jo's belongings?"

"Yes, sir," Fanny said. "I've been staying with my sister, but I'm gonna need money."

"I'll get that sorted next week," Carlyle replied. "Make sure you leave nothing behind. I think this will be the only time we're allowed in, and it's entirely possible that this place could be ransacked some more or even burnt down. I'll let Jo know her stuff is in storage." He led the way downstairs and paused in the hallway to look in the parlour. The walls and floor were slathered in axe marks or ripped away completely. "So goddamn despicable. We ready, ladies?"

They marched one by one out the doors and waited on the stoop for him to lock both. He pocketed the keys and helped them into their taxi, told the movers where to take the furniture and other items, and then climbed into his car and left the brownstone, unaware of all eyes on him.

The man stood across the road, under the tree that was behind a car. He'd been watching a while, walking up and down the street hoping to see something that would give him a clue. But all he saw was slashed furniture being loaded into a moving van.

He wondered if he should try and get into the brownstone. There must be a back way. A back door. A back window. He needed to see for himself if the place was cleared out. He needed to see for himself if she had left anything behind. He walked down the road, turned the corner, and walked down the back lane towards her yard.

A man sat low in the driver's seat of his car, watching the other man walk off down the road. He'd seen him walking around and considered him just a fan of the madam's. But now he wondered if he was up to no good.

What if he's after her stuff? What if he's going to break in? It looks like he's casing the joint. Maybe I should've followed him? Is there a back way in? I used to enter and exit via the garage and an underground walkway. Maybe I can do that again? Would it be locked up tight? Would anything be left? She had three bolts on the back door. If they're in place, I can't get in. Damn! I wonder if she left anything?

After contemplating some more, he decided to take the back road behind her brownstone and see if the man was lurking around. He drove off, went around the block, and slowly cruised past the brownstone. He couldn't see anything, everything was black and no doubt locked up tight. But he would definitely be coming back another night.

*****

There were ten table setups and ten small seating sections in the room of the gentleman's club on Fifth. Four chairs were around each square table, and six chairs around each round coffee table.

The men all sat and stared at each other, glasses or cigars in hands.

Cyrus was the first to speak. "I cannot believe Eugene didn't let her go, and now he's dead. What's going to happen to us?"

Harlan puffed on his cigar and regarded his companions. Bernard, Howard, Cyrus, Donald and Benedict. "Well, that's what happens when you arrest a madam. You're exploits are going to become common knowledge. They should have just let her go."

"Does anyone know who arranged for the arrest?" Donald asked. "Judge, mayor, politician. Who?"

Bernard shook his head. "Haven't heard anything. Everyone's staying silent."

"They should. Or they'll get their faces splashed across the papers from the west coast to the east coast." Howard finished his drink and set the glass down on the coffee table. He was thoughtful. "Do we know who it *could* have been?"

"Someone who didn't go to her," Benedict suggested. "Someone with nothing to lose."

"We've all got something to lose." Harlan puffed his cigar and blew smoke rings. "I may have my magazine empire, and it's entirely possible nothing would happen to me because of it. But the rest of you, especially lawyers, politicians, judges. Naughty, naughty."

"I can't believe Eugene's dead," Cyrus repeated. He was dazed, still in shock. "She was arrested Sunday, the hearing was yesterday, and Everett recused himself and Eugene dropped dead of a heart attack today. How is that even possible?"

"It's entirely possible, as we've seen. And we're only Tuesday," Howard said. "But if she's got proof, how is she getting it to the Press? Is it through her lawyer? Someone else? Does someone have copies of the photos? Is it the girls. I bet it's them wanting to make money from this. They wouldn't be getting paid by Jo anymore, it must be the girls. I bet they took photos for blackmailing purposes in case something like this ever happened."

"Considering what Bartie did, I don't think that's something any of us want coming out." Benedict frowned and let the last drop of cognac slide down his throat. "None of us want that coming out. We were there that night. We would all be implicated."

"Bartie's dead. I wonder if anyone's connected the dots?" Donald asked.

"Not unless someone's very smart and has knowledge of the inner workings," Harlan replied. "Like Cormac Ryan."

Everyone looked at him. "You don't think Cormac's behind this?" Cyrus asked.

Harlan glanced at him. "He *is* the commissioner. But I also reckon that Allan Gerard is in on it."

"The mayor?" Bernard frowned in thought. "Why would he—"

"*Because* he's the mayor and wants to be voted back in, so he wants to be seen as doing *something* to clear up the prostitution he's allowed to go on for so long. I also think Bartie's wife wormed her way into his ear. Especially after what Jo did to her at the funeral."

They were silent for a while, waved over the waiter for another round of drinks, and thought about the trial that would start on Monday.

Finally, Cyrus asked, "So, does anyone know of a good madam who won't tell our secrets? Jo kept them to herself, they never left her lips."

Everyone shook their head.

"No. But how the hell are we going to replace her?" Bernard asked.

Harlan grinned. "Maybe you little pussies should go and have a chat to the mayor. Bernard, Cyrus, you're politicians. Benedict, you're a lawyer. Go and have a chat and heavy hand him into paying for the house to be redecorated and her to be reinstated. Otherwise, information on him just might turn up in the Press."

Chapter 9

"Oh, ma'am, I cannot believe you're in here." Hilda nervously glanced around at the other inmates at the remand centre family room. "Why haven't they freed you yet?"

Josephine sighed. "I have no idea, Hilda. I was kept in remand thanks to Eugene, and then Judge Crawford, whom I've never heard of. I really wish I'd been allowed to go home, but then home has been confiscated and trashed. She said keeping me in was for my safety. At least I've been left alone. For the most part." She looked at the two guards by the door. "They have orders from the judge to make sure I'm kept safe and be allowed visitors and a few things in my cell." She leaned forward for news. "How *is* my house? Was it really bad?"

"Oh, ma'am, it was horrendous." Hilda clutched her hands together in front of her. "The floors need replacing, the wall panelling that Ms Ryan did all those years ago, the beautiful wallpaper, all completely trashed. Mr Houston had all of the furniture packed up and put in storage, and Fanny, Myrtle and I wrapped up what we could find of yours from your mother and grandmother.

Sadly, the china was almost demolished and the crystal beyond repair. But we wrapped it up carefully and put it all in separate boxes in a bigger box. It's clearly marked. So is your clothing and personal items they didn't take. We have some clothing for you which we were told you would need. I had to leave it at check-in."

Josephine gazed down at her orange jumpsuit. "At least I'll have clothing for the trial next week. My poor dress that I was wearing upon arrest is now worse for wear."

Hilda looked at her mistress. "Are they treating you well, ma'am? Is there something I can do? Has anyone else come to see you? Fanny and Myrtle wanted to come with me, but we weren't sure how many were allowed to visit you at the one time. Can they come and see you?"

Josephine's lips flattened into a tight smile. "Best not, Hilda. It might make things even more complicated, especially for the three of you. Stay where you are and stay safe." She paused. "Let's talk business a moment. Am I to presume that all *parties* were cancelled."

"Yes, ma'am." Hilda nodded. "Phone calls were made to those who had appointments and everything cancelled. Mr Houston took charge of everything else."

"What about the garden?" Josephine's far away gaze meandered up to the ceiling. "My poor garden. It needs nourishment and care, who's going to take care of it now?"

"Don't know, ma'am. Rocco could if he was allowed onto the premises."

They chatted about a few personal things before Hilda bade her goodbye.

"Do be careful, Hilda, stay safe." Josephine smiled at

her, unable to give her housekeeper a goodbye hug. "I'll see you the next time you come in."

"Oh, I won't be able to this week, ma'am. But I will be there next week to support you." Hilda smoothed her three quarter houndstooth coat and straightened the matching hat with its maroon plume of feathers on the right side. "We'll definitely be there next week."

"I'll see you next week then. My love to the others." Josephine watched her leave and let out a sigh. This week was going to be painful to deal with.

As the remand centre had relaxed rules, Josephine wandered back to her cell to finish the book she'd been reading. She had only just started chapter nine when a guard leaned into her cell. "Another visitor, Madam. I'll take you back to the family room."

Surprised, Josephine followed him back to the room to see Portia waiting for her. "Well, hello, darling. What are you doing here?" She took a seat opposite her at the table. "What's going on? Has something happened?"

Portia leaned towards her and whispered, "Of course something's happened, Madam, we're all out of a job and worried we'll be arrested next."

Josephine nodded. "I understand how you could think that, but Carlyle assured me nothing would happen."

"Sorry, Madam, I don't trust lawyers. Look what one did to you. Threw you in jail and now we're out of a job. The other girls and I got together and they picked me to be the leader. They wanted me to come in to see what was going on, and what would happen to us."

Josephine sighed and rested her chin on her hand. "I know. But the honest answer is, I *don't know.* I have no clue how the trial will go next week. I have no idea how long it will take, or whether I'll be found guilty or not guilty, and in that case, how much time I'll serve. But I've spoken to Carlyle, which seems to be all I'm doing, and he knows to make sure everyone gets a weekly wage. If I am sentenced, then you'll get two month's severance. That's all I can afford to give if I won't be out and running my business."

Portia frowned and leaned back in her seat. "So, we'll get a weekly wage until you go to jail and then two months wage. What do we do about jobs?"

Josephine was sympathetic. "Portia, if I'm jailed, there *is* no business to run which means you girls will have to put your own plans in motion if the verdict to send me away comes down. Whether that means you finish your schooling and get your degrees, or start up small businesses, or go back to school, then it has to be done. I helped you all with your future plans when you came to work with me. I didn't want this to be your forever career. There's so much more out there for you. If I'm sentenced to prison, go and get on with your lives."

Portia pursed her lips and nodded. "I get what you're saying, Madam, but what if we can't? Some of the girls want to keep working in the field. Where are they supposed to go?"

Josephine shrugged. "I can hardly give you all resumes and recommendations, now can I? Look…" She wished she could lean over and hold her hands, but even in the family room, touching was not allowed. "If I get out, I'll see if I can restart. But considering they completely trashed my house, I don't know how long that would take to repair and I've been thinking for some time that I would retire at seventy-five. That's three years away. The house could take that long to refurbish. Then what? It's time for retirement. So maybe this is a good thing. It forces our hands where our plans are concerned. It's time you girls get on with your lives, and I'll see what happens to mine with this trial."

Portia put her elbows on the table and rested her chin in her hands. "Madam, do you think they'll find you guilty?"

"Aren't I?" Josephine cocked a brow. "Judge Crawford most likely will, considering she's a woman and I have nothing on her. *Eugene* on the other hand, I had plenty on, but can't use it. Which is surprising…" She leaned back in her seat and mused on that thought. "Someone made him sign the warrant. Something made him refuse to recuse himself. I wonder who, and what." She turned her attention back to Portia. "Have any of the girls been contacted by anyone?"

A child visiting their mother across the room screamed and Portia jumped in her skin. "Who? Who would contact us?"

Oh, I don't know…" Josephine mused, a conspiratorial grin on her lips. "Lawyers, judges, the FBI, CIA, the Mayor, the Commissioner, anyone higher up."

Portia shook her head. "No, not that I know of. I certainly haven't been. Would we even be that easy to find?"

"I'm sure they could get anyone's phone or address. Plenty of men in high positions came to see you girls. They could tell them what you looked like, your names. They could have staked out the house to take photos of you coming and going."

"What!" Portia shot up ram-rod straight. "They've been stalking us? Who?"

Josephine shrugged. "Anyone, everyone. If they're out to get me, P, then they could be out to get you girls. Stay safe, stay under the radar, stay out of the limelight and off the streets. Who knows who could pick you up if you decided to take to the streets and pick up johns. You could all be dead in no time. Stay low, keep your heads down, don't come to the trial, stay out of the way and out of the Press and you should be okay. Carlyle has a list of your names and numbers. He'll contact you about your wages once my accounts are unfrozen."

Portia gulped and clutched her bag to her chest. "Are we safe, Madam?"

"Keep your head down and you will be, P." Josephine smiled at her. "Tell the girls the same. Tell them to get on with their careers. Harmony and Heaven won't get to, but all of you should."

Portia cocked her head. "What do you mean by that? Didn't Harmony and Heaven leave to pursue their degrees?"

Josephine's expression fell. "Sadly, no, thanks to Bartie Winthrop. But no more talk of that. Don't worry, just stay safe and get on with it."

*****

Bernard Dietrich walked into Allen Gerard's office.

"Bernard."

"Allen."

They shook hands and Allen offered him a drink.

"No, thank you, not at this time of the day. But feel free."

The mayor replaced the crystal decanter of bourbon on his drinks trolley and shrugged. "So, what did I do to deserve a visit from one of New York's highest ranking politicians?" Allen walked around his desk and motioned to the chair opposite it. "Take a seat." He sat and got comfortable.

"Josephine Pompadour."

Allen stared at him, his heart thudding in his chest at the mere mention of the name. "What about her?"

"Get her out of jail, Allen. It was you, wasn't it?" Bernard crossed his legs and stared Allen down. "You demanded for Cormac to arrest her for solicitation and prostitution, even though you know she could bring us all down. And we know you've been to see her, Allen. Do you really want to lose the mayorship over this woman?"

Allen's breath left him in a rush. "How do you…"

"We've seen you, you idiot." Bernard sighed and rubbed his tired eyes. "Eugene dropped dead of a heart attack after seeing his photo in the paper. Everett's wife threw him out, and now there's a bid for Alec Ryan to replace him. Another fucking Ryan in a head job of law enforcement. Like that's all we need." His arm dropped to his lap. "We're tired, Allen. Tired of the threat of our secrets coming out. Because if you don't stop this, there may be some behind the scenes manoeuvring to get you out. You started this, you need to finish it."

Allen huffed. "That would be all well and good if Eugene was still the judge, but Isadora Crawford is now and she's not about to budge on her stance. The trial starts Monday—"

"Then you'd better hope we're all safe, Allen," Bernard threatened. "You had better hope that Josephine doesn't reveal any more photos of who spent time in her home. Because hundreds of us would be screwed in more ways than one."

Allen's breath was shaky as he stared at Bernard. If anyone could do damage to his career, it was the man sitting across from him. "I can't change things now. Even if I wanted to."

"Which you don't because you started this in the first place," Bernard countered and stood up. "Beware, Allen. If this blows up in our faces, I'll make sure it blows up in yours and you are run out of town never to be mayor again. I'll see myself out." Closing the door behind him, he didn't see the scared expression on Allen's face, or see him pick up the phone.

"Cormac, I need to see you. My office, now." With a shaky hand, Allen set the phone back in its cradle. "What the fuck!" he muttered and ran his hands through his hair. He'd had Mary Winthrop in his ear about Josephine Pompadour and what was he going to do about her since Bartie's funeral. He'd also had pressure from higher-ups who'd been at the funeral. Someone needed to do something about Madam X and it was up to him. He'd argued back and forth with Everett, telling him that it would set them all on the trail to destruction none of them would able to come back from. And now it looked like that destruction had started with Eugene *and* Everett. *And* him.

"That backfired in his face, the stupid bastard. Demanded I do something about Josephine and then he's the second one to fall. Goddam it. Who's going to be next?" He paced around his office waiting for Cormac, and when he entered, he locked the door behind him.

"I've just had a visit from Bernard Dietrich, demanding I fix this Madam X Josephine Pompadour case." Allen sat behind his desk and stared at Cormac. "He knows I'm behind it and suggested it was because Mary was in my ear."

"Was she? Apart from at the funeral?" Cormac asked, adjusting his blazer. "Is this what you called me in for?"

"Of course it's what I called you in for," Allen shouted, and with a scared glance at the door, lowered his voice. "It's the only bloody thing this town is talking about. Madam X, Josephine Pompadour and her prostitution ring out of her brownstone. And then there's Eugene and Everett, and now Bernard's in my office telling me to fix it or someone's going to fix me."

Cormac's furry brows dipped. "Fix you how?"

Allen cleared his throat. "That they would make sure I lose my job, the way Everett will most likely lose his. To your son," he said pointedly. "I do not want to be blackballed from the mayorship because of this woman. We need to stop this trial, or make sure she never tells anyone who else visited her."

"And how would we do that? Isadora Crawford is one hell of a judge; she won't easily stop this trial."

"We could drop all charges against Josephine, and then she'd have to walk free."

"Isadora will question that."

Allen waved a frustrated hand. "I don't care. I've been informed that there are many men who don't want this getting out, and I have to do something."

"Or how about you do nothing, and let her go to jail?"

Allen saw his slimy smile under his thick moustache. It was as thick as his brows and looked weird above his lip. "Did I ever tell you you remind me of Oscar the grouch?" He waved another hand. "But I digress. I need to stop this, but unless I drop all of the charges, which I don't think I can, it won't. Who drops charges around here?"

"The DA's office. But, since Everett's in trouble…"

"Damn it!" Allen growled. "Any other bright ideas? What about your son?"

Cormac frowned in confusion. "Which one?"

"Alec, of course. If he's going to be the next DA then he can get her out."

"Well, I have no idea if he's going to be or not, and even then, it could take weeks if not months for that process, so don't rely on him."

Allen threw his hands up in frustration, then stormed to his feet and roamed the office. "What the fuck am I going to do?"

"Talk to the DA's office, strongly suggest this be dropped."

"Great idea. Everett can't be the only one in that office who saw Madam X and her girls."

Cormac blanched, grateful that Allen was somewhere behind him. "Who knows how many men have been to see Josephine. Maybe we should seriously rethink this court case."

"So then I have to talk to the DA's office and find out who's taken over the case."

"That would be Georgia Pérez, at the moment."

"Damn, another woman." Allen slumped back into his chair and nibbled at his thumbnail. "A female attorney and judge. I don't think this is going to be dropped easily."

"Then there's not much I can do. I just made the arrest based on your warrant that was signed off by Eugene Haskell." Cormac rose to his feet. "Unless there's something else?"

Allen waved him off. "No. I'll get in contact with the DA's office and see what I can do. Unless I follow this through and let it happen."

Cormac sighed and turned for the door. "Not unless you want hundreds of prominent men in New York to be after your hide. Goodbye, Allen. Nice knowing you." He closed the door after him, and left to see his son. Fifteen minutes later, he sauntered into his son's office.

"Dad, to what do I owe this pleasure?" Alec sorted some files on his desk.

Cormac locked the door and walked over to him. "Allen Gerard and Josephine Pompadour."

Alec looked at him in interest. "I know about the case, but what's Allen got to do with it?"

"He's the one who filed the charges and had me arrest her. Now he's been threatened and wants to back out. With Everett in trouble and most likely not keeping his DA role, that means you could be the next District Attorney and he wants you to sort this out. But as I told him, that could take weeks, if not months." Cormac settled into the brown leather wingback chair at the desk. "Allen's worried about his career and position. It's been threatened."

"By whom?" Alec leaned back in his chair. "Who threatened

him, and how could he bring charges against her. What the hell's going on here?"

"I don't know." Cormac sighed and tapped his fingers on the chair arm. "He filed the charges, got Haskell to sign off on them, but then look what happened to him. Now Allen's scared that he'll end up in the paper thanks to Josephine, and Bernard Dietrich has told him to get it sorted or lose everything."

"Bernard…Dietrich." Alec mused. "Interesting that a highly regarded and upstanding politician is getting involved."

"Just goes to show how many people are involved," Cormac replied. "Hundreds."

"If not thousands," Alec murmured, and remembered back to the times he'd visited Madam X's. That's how he met Sonja. Something no one could find out about. "We need to do something about this. Either get the office to drop the charges or make sure Josephine never talks again."

Cormac regarded his son. "And how do you plan on doing that?"

Alec shrugged. "I'll have a chat to the higher-ups here. You go and have a chat to Madam X and tell her to keep her mouth shut. She revealed those photos of Eugene and Everett, who knows who'll she reveal next."

"Yeah…" Cormac muttered. "Who knows."

*****

Sonja Ryan waited nervously in the remand centre's family room for Josephine. She had donned a brunette wig, round framed glasses, and wore dowdy clothes. There was no way in all of hell she wanted to be recognised in that place, so she had flashed illegal identification at the officer when she entered. She saw Josephine enter and waved.

Puzzled by the sight of a woman she didn't recognise, Josephine walked over and sat down, peering at her new companion. "And who are you?"

She leant forward and whispered furtively, "It's me, Sonja."

"Ryan?" Josephine asked in surprise. "My, my, this is…unexpected."

Sonja's gaze darted around the room. "I wasn't sure I should come. I shouldn't be here, but I needed to know what's going to happen?"

"Concerning what?" Josephine took in her appearance. "You obviously don't want anyone knowing you're here. Do you not want anyone knowing you renovated my brownstone? Well, Alec and Cormac already know that. I'm sure many other people do too."

"No, it's not about the renovations. It's about…" Sonja glanced around. "The other thing. I can't have that getting out."

"Oh…" Josephine's brows rose and she leaned back in her seat. "I see. Worried that all names will come out, are you? Worried about yours, or Alec's? Cormac's or Douglas's?"

Sonja's eye grew wide in alarm. "What? Cormac and Douglas? Oh, my God." She shook her head to clear it. "No, me and Alec. It would ruin the careers we've both acquired since. I need to know that you're not going to say anything, and it's not going to get out. Like with that judge and the DA."

Josephine raised her hands in surrender. "I haven't said anything. The only people I've talked to in the last few days has been my lawyer, the staff here, and all of my visitors. I didn't release anything to the Press. Why do you all think I'm stupid? I don't want to ruin my career any more than all of yours. And my lawyer certainly didn't reveal anything to the Press, so I'd say that someone else knows something. Maybe one of the men did it. I wouldn't put it past them if they use the trial to get back at each other. Those men always did behave like children depending on who got which girl, and who got which room to do that girl in. Maybe it was one of the girls, but I highly doubt that. They wanted their jobs, and their privacy. Who knows who it could be."

"Please promise me you won't reveal anything else," Sonja pleaded.

"I didn't reveal anything in the first place," Josephine replied, insulted. "I have said nothing to no one, but unless you want someone to take a wild guess at who you are, I suggest you go and tell your father-in-law that my lips are sealed. Did he send you here, or did you come off your own back?"

Now Sonja was insulted. "I came here to tell you to keep your mouth shut," she muttered through gritted teeth. "I can't have people knowing about me. Say nothing." She shoved up from her chair and glowered down at Josephine. "Say nothing."

"I never said anything in the first place." Josephine glared after her as she stormed through the door. "I wonder if I should now."

*****

Sonja sped her way to the district attorney's building and took the lift up to her husband's office. She had left the wig and glasses in the car, along with the dowdy outfit she'd had on over her good clothing. Barging into Alec's office she slammed and locked the door. "Alec, we need to talk."

Alec held his hand up to stop her. "Yes, sir, I understand… No, I completely understand. I'll do it right away… Of course. Thank you, sir." He hung up the phone and stared thoughtfully out the floor-to-ceiling windows framing New York City.

"Alec!"

He turned to her. "Sonja, don't ever come screaming into my office making such a noise ever again. I was on the phone to the governor about taking over as the new district attorney. You could have ruined it."

"Josephine Pompadour could ruin more." Sonja slumped into the chair at his desk. "I just went to see her. She claims she didn't say anything about that judge and the DA and how their photos made their way into the papers. I don't know if I believe her."

"You went to see her? Why would you take such a risk? We can't have people knowing you know her?" Alec declared.

"Of course, people know I know her, I remodelled her brownstone years ago." Sonja threw up her hands and stalked over to the window. "I wanted to know if she'd keep her mouth shut about us and me working for her. She said she hadn't told anyone, and she'd only talked to her lawyer and the staff at the centre. Who could she have told? I told her to keep her mouth shut."

"Why are you threatening her?" Alec moved around his desk and leaned against it. "*Do not* make things worse for us, Sonja. We don't need our secrets coming out. Yours is bad enough, but if anyone found out about me, and then the kids, there would be hell to pay and all of our careers would be at stake."

Sonja glared coolly at her husband. "Oh, and who's all? You and me? You, me, your father and grandfather? Considering they went to Josephine as well."

Alec stepped back in shock. "What? What do you mean Dad and Pop went to her? You can't be serious?"

"Oh, I'm very serious considering she said it me. And yes, I was just as shocked as you are. Are their careers going to be ruined if our secrets get out? Is that who you meant?"

Alec smoothed the lapels of his light grey suit jacket. "Yes, Sonja," he said quietly. "It would ruin *all* of our careers and I will not do that to my father or grandfather. You and I losing our jobs is one thing, but my father's job, and my grandfather's reputation is another. Not to mention what it would do for the family to know their niece and nephew aren't even related to them. So you'll stay silent, and I'll work on making sure Josephine Pompadour does as well."

Chapter 10

"Pop, you home?"

"In here."

Cormac walked into the sun room of his house and saw his father sitting by the open French doors watching the dying rays of the sunset. "We have a problem."

Douglas watched his son's weary face. "And what problem would that be?"

"An Allen Gerard, Josephine Pompadour problem." Cormac sat heavily in his leather chair and sighed. "The mayor called me in today to talk about Josephine and how he could stop the trial from happening. He's been threatened."

"By whom?" Douglas sat up and became interested. "Why would he want to cancel the trial?"

"Apparently Bernard Dietrich has threatened him. Wants him to drop the charges and call it off. If he doesn't, he may no longer be mayor of New York."

"Fascinating," Douglas murmured and stroked his chin. "Dietrich is a bigwig. That must mean there's a lot at stake on this."

"That's why I warned Allen from doing it in the first place. There's too many careers that can be damaged or ruined. But he insisted that he was getting pressure from higher up to do it, and that Mary Winthrop had been in his ear since the funeral. That's why he did it. He wasn't scared to file the charges, but now that other powers that be are coming down on him, he's freaking out."

"What do you think he'll do?"

Another sigh. "I think he'll try and get them dropped. But Isadora Crawford has taken over and set the trial for Monday. I don't think she'll back down from it and would need a good reason for stopping it."

"Isadora…" Douglas muttered. "The woman who took down the Muchacho mob ten years ago as the district attorney?"

"That's the one. She does not play nice, but she is fair as a judge."

Douglas stared out at the view. The lights displayed the city at its best as the sun finally dipped below the horizon ready to brighten up the other side of the planet. "It's Wednesday. Do you think he'll do it? As much as I wanted her arrested…"

"And made a big deal out of it," Cormac replied. "We all knew the risk of arresting her for no good reason, and Eugene and Everett have been the first victims of it. We could all fall down one by one like toy soldiers, so you'd better prepare for it, Pop."

Douglas looked at him. "So should you."

Cormac nodded gravely. "I know. I know. I can only hope Allen can actually do something."

*****

Allen walked into Isadora's chambers, catching her just as she was getting ready to leave. He locked the door. "We need to talk."

Surprised, she paused and dropped her bag back on her desk. "About, Mr Mayor?"

Allen strode over to her desk. "Josephine Pompadour."

"And what about it? The trial starts on Monday."

He took a breath and let it out slowly. "I know I brought the charges, but now I want them dropped."

She cocked her head in interest. "Why?"

"Because I didn't realise that Eugene would drop dead, and Everett would be ousted as district attorney. There are consequences to this trial I did not anticipate. I need it to be stopped and Josephine Pompadour to be set free."

Isadora crossed her arms and took a moment to compose herself, steeling herself against the mayor. "I won't be doing any such thing. You filed charges, Eugene signed off on them. It's now my case and I plan on prosecuting it."

"Then be prepared to lose your job," he told her. "Just as I will. Just as many other judges will, lawyers and cops will, politicians will."

Her arms dropped to her side. "Are you saying this is coming from higher up?"

He nodded. "For me, yes. I have been told to stop it. So now I need *you* to stop it."

"Or what?" She walked around to desk and stood toe to toe with him. "Are *you* threatening me? Are *they* threatening me?"

"Not at the moment," he relied smoothly. "But they are threatening me and now I'm telling you to drop this trial and let her go."

"Or?"

"Or you may no longer be a judge."

Isadora stared deeply into his eyes and saw a level of fear. "Unlike you, Allen, I don't scare easily. I'm not dropping this case just because you changed your mind."

"It's not a matter of me changing my mind, it's a matter of me keeping my job," he said honestly. "I didn't take into account how many people would be affected because I let a few get into my head. And now those who *will* be affected are coming down on me. Setting Josephine free won't hurt anyone and we all get to keep our jobs. Including you."

"Is that an underhanded threat?"

"No." He sighed. "Just the truth. Let her go, Isadora. For all our sakes."

*****

Carmelo finished up with the street hooker and tucked himself away. He hated fucking some strange chick in an alley, especially after tasting the girls at Madam X's. But thanks to her being in jail, and the trial and all, which he was constantly over thanks to the TV news and papers talking about it daily, he had no one else to go to who would keep his identity quiet.

He knew a few guys who had gone to other madams, but their names had gone around to pimps, and then the pimps were coming to them to try out their girls. He didn't like that. Didn't want his name being passed around to those who controlled the girls. He just wanted the privacy of the brownstone.

"Fuckin' cops had to arrest her," he muttered, pulling out a twenty from his wallet. He threw it at her. "Here, get out of here. That was pathetic."

She snatched the note. "You're rippin' me off. I said forty, you owe me another twenty, mothafucka. And considerin' you shoved it up my ass and it hurt like hell, no wonder it was pathetic. You some fag or somethin'? Only fags fuck like that."

His hand cracked across her cheek and she spun into the wall, covering her face. He stood over her, thrusting his right forefinger at her. "Don't you ever say shit like that again, you got me? I ain't no fag. I don't fuck men. Now get outta here you fuckin' whore."

She pulled her fake fur coat around her and used the wall to lean against as she climbed to her feet. "I ain't no whore," she yelled, and ran off down the alley, teetering in her tatty heels. "Fuckin' fag!" She ran around the corner and out of sight before he could go after her.

"I ain't no fuckin' fag!" he yelled, hands clenched into fists at his side before he slammed one into a wall. "Ah, fuck it!" He doubled over in pain and gripped his hand. "Fuck you, you whore! I wouldn't have to fuck you, you whore, if Madam X still had her house. I'd still be usin' her girls and not havin' to fuck the likes of you. Ah." He shook his hand and noted the blood in the faint lamplight. "Fuck it. Maybe I should do somethin' about it. Get back at the fuck who had her arrested and ruined it for everyone." He remembered back to the last time he was there, when he'd fucked one of her girls up the ass, and then remembered Madam X had shoved a gun in his face and banned him from her establishment. "Fuckin' whore, you're exactly where you need to be. Fuckin' bannin' me from fuckin' your girls. Fuck you. Maybe I should set up my own whore house and take her girls away." The idea formed in his head and he grinned. "Yeah, yeah, that's a good idea. I can take all the girls I want and form my own whore house. And then take out the pimps, and deal with the trash." He nodded enthusiastically at his plan. "Yeah, yeah, that's a good one."

*****

The man snuck across the back yard, down the basement stairs, and tried the door. "Damn it. Locked." He peered over the steps into the yard to see if anyone was around, and hurried up to the back door, trying the handle. "Damn it!"

He moved along the terrace and found a window that was unlocked. Lifting it, he launched himself through and into the kitchen.

"Okay, let's see what's left."

Initiating a thorough search of each room, he pulled out his flashlight and made good time. The kitchen, library, parlour, plus the small lavatory all held no secrets. He peered into the wall and floor cavities, before heading up to the second floor where he found four bedrooms. The furniture had been removed, like downstairs, and nothing was left, so he checked the floor and walls cavities in each room.

"They really did a number on this house," he muttered, and headed up to the next floor. He found them barren of everything, and the small shared bathroom held no secrets. He moved up to the top floor he knew was purely for the madam and made good time ploughing through the bedroom and small bathroom. Again, the rooms had been emptied of furniture and personal effects, so there was nothing to really search. But he added to the mess made by the cops and pulled more wall tiles off in the bathroom, and more floor panels up in the bedroom.

After half an hour, he found nothing and made his way down to the basement where he found the three extra bedrooms. "Interesting…" He searched all three and went into the laundry room where there was nothing. He flashed his light into the small room where he found the toilet, and moved onto the large room that was devoid of everything. "This was the sex room. They took everything."

Sighing, he ran his hand along the concrete wall. Nothing had been damaged in there, but most other rooms had been. He walked out and stood staring around. "So where would she have hidden her client list? This little black book I've heard rumours about. Where could it be? With her lawyer? Highly possible. Hidden from view? Also possible. Does someone else have it? Possibly, if they stole it, like the cops who stormed in and took everything. Either way, I'm clearly not finding anything."

He hurried upstairs, switched off his torch, and slid out through the kitchen window, sliding it down before dashing away into the night.

*****

"Jo, how are you holding up?" Carlyle asked as Josephine walked into the small room he'd sequestered at the remand centre to speak to his client. "It's Friday, only two more days before the trial starts. How do you feel?"

"How do you think I feel? Like a prisoner." She motioned to her jumpsuit. "I'm wearing an ugly outfit, I'm confined to prison. How am I supposed to feel?" Josephine took her seat and sighed. "Get me out of here, Carlyle."

He took the seat opposite. "I'm doing my best, Jo, but it's not easy. I'm filing petitions, and have asked to speak to the judge. She denied my request. I spoke to Allen Gerard on Monday about dropping the charges. No go. Then he called me up yesterday and told me he was trying to get them dropped, but Crawford was saying no."

"Allen," Josephine scoffed. "He started this, that dumb fuck can finish it. Tell him to get me out of here or he'll be next to go."

Carlyle smirked. "He spoke to Crawford, she's adamant that she's not dropping this, so it's not going to matter who talks to her."

"And I don't have any dirt on her." A thought occurred to her. "Unless…"

"Unless?"

"Unless she worked for my mother, at one point," Josephine replied. "She certainly didn't work for me, but she may have worked for my mother or someone else. I don't have those books, obviously, but maybe you can find something in them about her."

"I do have your mother's belongings in my care. I can certainly look for her name, and see what other dirt I can find on her that I could use. Maybe she has secrets of her own. But until then, let's get on with prepping for this trial."

"I can't believe there's going to be a trial," Josephine muttered. "What the hell happened for this to have reached this point?"

"Mary Winthrop."

Josephine's gaze turned to Carlyle. "Mary? What? How?"

"A little birdy told me she was in Allen's ear about you after the funeral. Plus, a few other people who aren't clients of yours, decided to put pressure on the mayor to file charges and have you arrested. The threats from them spurred Allen into action. However, I think there have now been even more threats to get him to stop."

"Interesting," Josephine muttered. "That bitch needs to learn a lesson."

"She probably thinks the same thing about you, which is why she wormed her way into Allen's ear, and probably a few other ears of influential people."

"The ones who told him to arrest me?"

"They're the ones."

Josephine deflated with a sigh, and rested her chin in her hands. "This is all so tiring."

"I know, but hopefully, next week, I can make it be all over."

She nodded. "Get into my mother's books and see if you can find some dirt on her, or from anywhere else. Let's take her down."

*****

On Monday morning, Carlyle and Josephine rose behind the defence table and waited while Crawford took her seat.

"This is day one of the Josephine Pompadour Madam X trial. We have Carlyle Houston defence attorney, and Georgia Pérez prosecutor. Be seated."

They took their seats and the proceedings got underway, but not for long as they were interrupted by a clerk who strode through the judge's door and up to the box. He handed her a yellow A4 envelope and rushed away.

Crawford frowned, opened the envelope and looked inside. Intrigued by the paperwork, she pulled it out. Her face paled as she read the words and saw the names at the bottom of the paper. She shoved them back into the envelope and gazed around the courtroom in a daze, until her gaze landed on Carlyle and Josephine who had a sly grin on her face. "I don't know what you did, but I have been removed from this case. So you will be remanded in custody until this case can be sorted out and a new judge brought in." She banged her gavel. "Court dismissed. Take her away."

Josephine rose and glared back at Isadora until the guards removed her from the court. Carlyle followed and they were taken to a small room to await her removal.

"Well," he said when they were left alone. "That was eventful."

"Very. But the problem now is, how long am I going to be in remand, and who's the next judge? Can we get someone we can blackmail?"

"Probably not. After Eugene, no one's going to want to take this case. Least of all those who went to you. Isadora didn't, so she was going to be, hopefully, reasonable and fair."

"I wonder what it was in the envelope that spooked her so. Did you see how pale she went. She said she'd been removed. Interesting. So what now? What do we do now?" Josephine slowly paced the room. "How long am I going to be in remand? Will I even get a trial? Will I ever be released?"

"I have no idea, considering what's happening, but I have a really bad feeling they're going to drag this out." Carlyle slumped into one of the chairs. "We need to talk strategy for getting you out instead of just blackmailing everyone."

"No one's blackmailing. I've not opened my lips. I've spoken to you, my housekeeper, some of my girls, and Sonja Ryan in the remand centre. I've made no calls and taken no calls—"

"Wait…"He stopped her with an outstretched hand. "Did you say you've spoken to Sonja Ryan? Why? When?"

Josephine paused her pacing. "Oh, Tuesday, I think it was. Maybe Wednesday. She came in wearing a disguise, no doubt with a fake ID."

"What did she want?"

"To ask if I was going to mention her. I said I had no intentions of mentioning anyone, but the Ryan family should be careful. Not a very long conversation."

"Why should they be careful?"

Josephine cocked her head at him and the corner of her lip lifted into a smirk. "Several generations have been to my brownstone. Not just Sonja when she redecorated."

Carlyle took in her words and got the gist of her meaning. "Wow. And he had the gall to arrest you and slap you, and his father had the gall to turn up demanding to talk to you. What did he want to know?"

"Where the client list was. The rumour was I had one. I lied and said there was no such thing and I didn't know what he was talking about."

"There is, obviously."

Josephine's grin spread across her face. "Of course there is."

The door burst open and Crawford strode in. "We need to have a little chat." She closed the door and slapped the papers down on the table. "How did you find this out, and who decided to use it against me?"

Carlyle picked the papers up and read through them. "Ouch. That's bad. But considering the names at the bottom, it clearly wasn't us." He handed them to Josephine.

Josephine read the letter and the signatures. "Very powerful men told you to drop this case or face disbarment. That's a lot. But then again, we all have secrets to hide, Isadora." She handed the papers back. "Why would it have to do with us when our names are not on the list."

Isadora snatched the papers back. "Don't think I don't know what you did. You set this up, somehow."

"Isadora," Josephine snapped. "You being an escort forty-five years ago to pay your way through law school is none of my business. You didn't work for me or my mother, but clearly men in power either used you, or remember you. And *clearly* they don't want this case going to trial. So what's happening? Am I being released, or are you still going to hold me in remand?"

Crawford studied them both and finally let out a whoosh of air. "You'll stay in custody and the trial can be reset. I'm not dropping this case—"

"Someone else will, it may be easier before it starts," Carlyle interrupted.

"Considering I've been threatened," Isadora spat, "I'll leave it to them to deal with it. And if they dare try and take me down, I'm taking them with me. They're not the only ones who can dig up dirt." She stormed out of the room, slamming the door behind her.

"Well, well, well," Josephine muttered. "How the worm turns."

"But you're still in custody and I have no idea what to do next." Carlyle opened his briefcase. "You're being kept in remand. I can file an injunction for your bail and release until the trial is set, but they've rejected my every attempt at doing so."

"Try again. She's out, someone else will be in, it may work this time. Meanwhile, call my friend and tell them to send a present to Allen Gerard. It might get a fire up his butt. Who else do we need to send a present to?"

*****

Carlyle went back to his office after Josephine was removed from the courthouse and made the call on a private phone.

An hour later, an A4 yellow envelope quietly turned up on Allen's desk while he was out.

When he returned, he saw it front and centre with his name on it. "What's this?" He opened it and pulled out the photos of him in a threesome with two of Madam X's girls. "Fucking Christ!" He shoved them back into the envelope, but a piece of paper snagged under them. He pulled it out and read the note. *Mr Mayor, if you don't have the charges against Madam X dropped, these photos will make their way into the news world. What's it going to be?*

"God, fuck!" He collapsed into his chair, the note falling to his desk. "What the fuck? Who… What… What the fuck do I do? How…" He frowned. "Josephine's in jail. How can she send these? Is her lawyer doing the sending? Only he could if she's unable to."

He picked up the phone and called his assistant. "Get Carlyle Houston on the phone. Now!"

He paced in front of his window while waiting, and two minutes later his phone buzzed. "Yes?"

"Allen, Carlyle. You want to speak to me?"

"Get over here now. I need to see you in person."

"For anything in particular?"

"You know damn well what for. Now, Carlyle."

Twenty minutes later, Carlyle waltzed into Allen's office. "Mr Mayor. How are we today?"

Allen rushed over to the door and locked it. Taking a breath, he spun around. "You know full well how I am. How do you have the photos? Who do you think you are sending them to me, threatening me with them?"

Carlyle cocked his head. "I have no idea what the hell you're going on about, Allen."

"These." Allen shoved the photos at him. "Where did you get these?"

Carlyle took them and flicked through. "Oh, Mr Mayor. Naughty, naughty. I have no idea where they came from, but they certainly didn't come from me. I have no such items."

"Someone does. That's taken in Josephine's brownstone.

Those girls are hers. Did she take photos? Videos? Is she sending them? Tell me!"

Carlyle threw them onto the desk. "First of all, Jo's in jail. Exactly how is she supposed to send you these photos? Second, today, we were in court for the first day of her trial, but that was cut short by the letter *you* sent Isadora Crawford." He saw the blood rush from Allen's face. "Yeah, she threatened us the same way you're threatening me and showed us the letter. We saw your name. Then, Josephine was taken back to the centre and I went back to my office. Exactly when was I, or Jo, supposed to send them to you?"

Allen slid into his chair. "Then who did? One of her girls?"

"What about one of the other men?" Carlyle suggested. "I know Harlan Conway took photos for himself. Josephine told me so. Maybe he's decided to get in on the threats and trial for some notoriety. An exposé for his trash rag."

Allen glanced up, his brows dipped into a deep v, and he realised he was in mortal danger of losing everything. "What's going on, Carlyle?"

Carlyle grinned. "All I can say, Allen, is that everyone who went to see Jo and her girls better watch out. If you're any part of her being in jail, you will be next. Because that's what this is beginning to look like. Someone has a vendetta, and it's neither me nor Jo, but someone *is* out to avenge her. Watch your back, Allen. And tell everyone else they should watch theirs. Someone is after those involved, and it's going to get messy if you don't do anything to stop it."

"So you do know!" Allen shot up out of his seat. "It *is* you."

"Don't be absurd, you stupid fool. Of course it's not. But it doesn't take a genius to see someone is out to get those involved in the arrest and trial of Josephine Pompadour. And since you started it all, you will no doubt be on the list. Watch your back, Allen. I know nothing about any of this, Jo has only seen me and four other people, and takes nor makes any calls. You can't prove she's doing anything, and I have no clue how these photos are getting out. I didn't even know they existed. So," he looked at his watch, "I have an appointment. All I can say, Allen, is get this dropped. I really don't see why it's so fucking hard to do so. You're the mayor, there are lawyers and judges involved, the district attorney has been dropped like a hot rock. Get off the train, Allen, because it's speeding up and there will be more casualties if you don't stop it."

Allen slammed his hands onto his desk. "You do know about these photos. You're the one sending them."

Carlyle sighed and rolled his eyes. "Get off the train, Allen. I just said, I have no idea where they're coming from, but anyone can see the train is going to crash and take mass casualties with it." He took a glance at the photos, shook his head in disgust, and left the room.

Chapter 11

The man jumped the back fence and ran full pelt to the back door. He tried it, but no luck. He hurried to the first window he came across and found it unlocked. Slowly lifting it to not create any noise, he jumped up and shimmied inside, finding himself in the kitchen.

He flicked on his torch and searched the room, but found nothing.

"Fuck it!" he muttered and hurried down the hall to the next room. The library. Bare wood floors and empty shelves that had been ripped apart by an axe. There was nothing to see. He hurried into the next room. The parlour was the same.

The muttering continued. "How am I supposed to find it if everything's gone?" He sighed, and quietly took the stairs up to the second floor where he explored the empty bedrooms. "She must have had someone come in and empty the place."

He moved up to the third floor and found two more bedrooms and a bathroom. Empty.

He moved up to the top floor, knowing it had been her room, and found nothing but holes in the floor and walls. He stuck his hands in each, hoping something had been left behind. "Where is it, where is it… Nothing. Damn it!"

He left the room and hurried down to the basement, searched each bedroom, the empty sex room, bypassed the toilet, and moved into the laundry. Not even that room had been spared from police axes.

He let out another sigh and leaned against the washing machine that had been left behind. There was nothing for him to find. "Where is it? He said she had one, she denied it, but it's gotta be here somewhere." He walked out of the laundry and stood staring at the layout of the basement. One large room for the sex room which was built under the garden. Small laundry and toilet on the opposite side. Three bedrooms had been erected in the large space left under the parlour and library above.

"They demolished every single room. Ripped up floorboards, tore down walls, trashed the furniture and nothing. So where the fuck is it?"

Heaving another sigh, he headed upstairs and stood in the parlour. Every man who came to Madam X would have sat in that room, on her furniture, drinking her alcohol, waiting for their girl to be available. "And now it's no more, thank God."

He made his way back to the kitchen and slid out the window, closing it behind him. Taking a quick look around for peering eyes, he ran for the back fence and silently jumped it before taking off down the road.

*****

Portia went to see Josephine on Tuesday morning.

"Madam, what's going on? We still haven't been paid and now your trial has been delayed. We saw it on the TV last night."

"Unfortunately, that is true," Josephine told her and looked around at the other people in the family room. Only three other inmates had visitors at that moment. "The judge was removed from the trial and I'm being held until there's a new judge willing to take it on, or someone drops all charges."

"Is your lawyer doing that? When will you be let out?" Portia tucked her hair behind her ears and furtively glanced around. She had once been in juvie for a couple of weeks and hated it, so being in the remand centre was freaking her out.

"No idea, my girl. Technically there is no reason to hold me. I haven't killed anyone, and while prostitution is illegal, it's not a good enough reason to keep me in. I could have been released on bail, but then where would I live?" Josephine shrugged. "I have no home, it's trashed. My assets are frozen, which means you won't get paid, but Carlyle's working on that, too. It's just been over a week, P, this will be sorted out and you'll be paid. But as I said last time, you girls need to start setting your plans in motion. Finish the degrees, set up your businesses. I've taught you all about finances since the day you started working for me. You should be okay for a while, especially if you get another job. Because I just have no idea what's going to happen at this point, or whether I'll bother going back to it once I get out."

"And when will that be?"

"No idea. I could be here for weeks or months. I could be let go and charges dropped, or sentenced to prison time. We have no idea."

Portia sighed and pulled her baggy sweater up around her neck, trying to hide inside of it for comfort. "I'll let the girls know. And I'll call Carlyle and see what's happening. I hope you stay safe, Madam. You mean a lot to us. You've been our surrogate mother."

Josephine flashed a small smile. "Thank you for those words, my girl. Let the others know I appreciate it *and* them. Stay safe, all of you, and stay off the streets."

Portia nodded and stood up, her gaze darting around. "I'll let them know. Bye, Madam."

"Goodbye, Portia." Josephine watched her leave, heaved a sigh, and went back to her cell which stayed open all day. She had her books to read, and notebooks to write in, hoping to retell her story from the inside. She needed to get it all out of her head for those who would come after her, needed her story to be known. But she knew that the guards would probably read what she was writing and if Carlyle was even able to get her effects to hand on, that would be a miracle.

There was one solid hope of protection, though. One of the guards had been a regular at the brownstone, so he made sure she was safe and her belongings kept where they were. He'd managed to tell her how pissed off he was that she'd been arrested and held in jail, and he would do what he could to help her.

She'd smiled warmly at him and given her thanks and that protection was still going on a week later.

She picked up her pen, opened to the next blank page

in her notebook, and began to write.

*****

Carmelo snorted through a line of coke, throwing his head back to let the rush overtake him. "Fuck yeah, man! That's some good shit." He leant down and snorted another line, then licked up what he hadn't snorted and collapsed back against the sofa. "Fuckin' good shit, man."

"You might want to save some for us," Benito said. "You also might want to cut back. You're snortin' more and more these days."

They were sitting around their headquarters getting high.

"Like I give a fuck, man. I got shit to do and shit to kill." Carmelo raised his hand to his forehead, fingers in the shape of a gun. "Pow, pow, pow, man."

"And who you gonna kill?" Enzio asked. He was slumped in an easy chair and smoking weed. He'd known Carmelo since he joined and had seen him kill Benecio. He also knew Carmelo was someone whose side he needed to be on.

"The mayor, man," Carmelo drawled, the high wafting him away. "That bastard shut down Madam X's. I was fuckin' the whores there until she banned me. And then she gets arrested before I can get back at her. Since she's in jail, I'll just kill him."

Enzio glanced at the others. "And how you gonna do that?"

"Been stalkin' him, man. I know where he goes on which nights."

"Tonight's Wednesday," Benito said. "Where's he at tonight?"

"Some fuckin' restaurant, man. I'm gonna go there and pow, pow, pow right in the kisser." Carmelo waved his gun-shaped hand around. "Pow, pow, pow."

Benito and Enzio exchanged a frown. If they let Carmelo do that, then their headquarters would be raided and they'd be sent to jail. And neither wanted to be sent back to jail.

"Why don't you sleep it off, man," Enzio suggested. "Tomorrow will be brighter and you'll want to do other things."

Carmelo waved him off. "Fuck off, man. I'm doin' it tonight." He launched himself up from the couch and checked his waistband for his gun. Its cartridge was full and he shoved it back in. "I'm gonna go and kill that mothafucka and teach him a lesson he won't soon forget." He staggered over to the table and grabbed the car keys and his jacket. "That mothafucka's goin' down."

Benito rushed over and grabbed his arm. "You ain't fit to drive, man, why don't you wait? You don't wanna get pulled over by the cops, do you?"

Carmelo shook him off. "Nah, man, I'll be fine. I know my way round this city like the back of my hand." He waved his right hand around in front of Benito's face. "I know which way to get there. I'll be fine." Swaying over to the car, he stumbled against it, then hauled himself up and waved his hand. "I'm good, man, just tripped on somethin'." He slid into the front seat and gunned the engine. This was gonna be good.

*****

Allen and his wife took their seats at the table. It was date night for the Gerards, and they always chose a different restaurant to dine in so they could sample all of New York. He felt, as the mayor, it was his duty to try out all of the city. *All* of the city.

He held the chair out for Cecily and waited for her to be seated before seating himself. As he whipped the napkin cross his lap he watched her. A striking woman in her fifties, she lived very much in the sixties. Her blonde bouffant hairdo was straight off of Marilyn Monroe, the fur stole, wrapped elegantly around her shoulders and over the body hugging white silk dress, was white mink, her skin an alabaster white to match.

Why the hell I'd ever think of cheating on her I have no idea, he thought. *Why the fuck would I do that? Maybe it's because our twenty-five year marriage is stale. And now look, there's going to be hell to pay.*

The waiter came over and he perused the wine menu. "We'll have the Bergerac Saussignac, thank you, and will order in a few minutes." He handed the menu back and smiled at his wife. "You look lovely as usual, my darling. Is that new?"

"What? The dress or the stole?" she asked in a smoky voice. A voice she knew drove him wild.

"Either. Both," he replied.

"Yes. To both." She grinned and laid her napkin across her lap. She was going to have to be careful with what she ordered tonight. Anything coloured would stain her outfit and she couldn't have that in New York. As the wife of the mayor, she needed to look her best at all times. That's why she had weekly beauty treatments, weekly shopping sprees, and weekly muscle strengthening. Exercise was not on her to-do list, but she needed to retain her figure which she did with pills and alcohol. Not very healthy, she knew, but then her workout trainer provided what she needed in every other area and he was *incredibly* healthy.

Allen smiled back and waited for the waiter to pour their drinks. "Is there anything in particular you'd like tonight? I don't think we've been here before."

"Nothing red. Keep it white. I don't want to stain my dress."

"Chicken or fish?" He read down the list of dishes.

"No fish. I don't want a bone in my throat. Chicken will do."

"Soup for an entrée?"

"Prawn cocktail, white sauce."

"And dessert?"

"Something white."

"Of course. White raspberry sorbet?"

"Too sugary."

"White cheesecake?"

"Too big. I'll take the sorbet if there's nothing else."

"Three course meal it is." Allen gave their orders and handed the menus back to the waiter. He waited until he was gone before putting his arms on the table and leaning towards his wife. "Tell me, darling, how's your week been so far?"

"Eventful." Cecily pulled a small compact mirror from her purse and checked her face for signs of oil. She dabbed the puff onto her nose and then closed the compact with a snap. "So far I've had my beauty treatment, my exercise treatment, and today my shopping treatment."

Allen nodded, knowing what the bill for all of those things was going to look like. "And tomorrow and Friday?"

"Oh, I'm sure I'll find some other treatment to have."

He ground his teeth. "I'm sure you will."

*****

Carmelo drove to the restaurant and parked haphazardly on the curb, drawing the attention of the passers-by. He slammed out of his car and up to the entrance, trying to make his way in. "I want the fuckin' mayor," he yelled to the maître d'. "Where's the fuckin' mayor?"

The manager and two security guards quickly approached.

"Sir, you are high or drunk and not welcome here," the manager told him while the guards took hold of both arms. "Please leave."

Carmelo scowled at the men on each arm and fought back. "I ain't leavin' till I see the fuckin' mayor. I know he's here. He was here last week."

"That was *last* week," the manager said as he was thrown out. "The mayor doesn't dine here every week. He and his wife try something different every Wednesday night. The police are on their way."

"Fuck the police," Carmelo yelled and managed to break free from the two guards. "An' fuck you." He flipped the bird with both middle fingers, ran to the driver's side and jumped in, roaring off down the street where took a left. If the mayor wasn't in that restaurant where the fuck was he? Heaving in breath like he'd run a thousand metre track, he pulled over to a side alley and calmed down. "If the fuckin' mayor's not there, then where the fuck is he?"

His phone rang and he fumbled in his back jeans pocket for it, seeing it was Benito calling. "Fuck you, man. I'd rather look through the internet." The light went off over his head. "I'll just fuckin' look for the cunt on social media." He scrolled through Facebook and Twitter for the mayor's pages and found he'd asked his followers on Facebook about a new restaurant he could try. He read through the replies and saw a comment from the mayor. *That sounds amazing. I'll give it a go.*

Carmelo smirked. "Gotch'ya!"

*****

Allen and Cecily were finishing up their meal. Small talk had been the talk of the day. Commenting on each meal, on Allen's work, their next dinner party, their next holiday.

Cecily finished off her wine and placed the glass on the table in front of her. Her fingers slid off the goblet, down the stem, and off the stand. "I do like that wine. We must have it again."

"At five hundred a bottle, I think that will be the only time we try it." Allen pulled out his card and handed it to the waiter who brought their bill. "A five hundred dollar bottle of wine is a bit steep for me."

"Not that you can't afford it." Cecily pulled out her compact and glanced at herself in the mirror. "I'm going to freshen up and then we can go."

"All right, my love." Allen stood up to pull out her chair. "I'll wait for you in the entrance hall." He followed her out of the restaurant and she went left to the ladies, he went right to wait by the door. He heard his phone ring and pulled it from his blazer's inside pocket. "Bernard. Why are you calling me?"

"Allen. You haven't dropped the charges against Josephine yet. Why not?"

Allen glanced around to see if anyone was nearby. "I tried. I sent Isadora that letter and she left the trial. But she remanded Jo in jail and is demanding the trial happen with another judge. I can't believe how hard this damn thing is to stop. It's like a runaway train that's speeding up."

"A train that none of us will be able to get off if you don't stop it now. I don't know why you started this, Allen. Threats from higher-up or not, you should have refused to do it and left it to someone else to be knocked off their pedestal. Because that's what's going to happen, Allen. You're going to be knocked off it and we'll all go to hell on that train. Get this trial stopped and over with. Talk to the DA and do it now. *Now.*"

The line went dead and Allen glanced at his phone before putting it away. He started pacing, thinking about the call.

In the bathroom, Cecily washed her hands and powdered her nose. She had managed to get not one stain on her white dress and stole and she was damn proud of it, as it would probably go back to the store next week. It would need a spritz under the arms, and an air out for the perfume, of course, but it was still in pristine condition. She smoothed the dress over her hips and wished she could keep it. But in order for her to save the stingy amount of money she received from Allen, she had to make sacrifices for her fashionable wardrobe so she wasn't seen in the same thing twice. Regardless of him paying the bills for the last twenty years, he'd constantly complained about the money she was racking up on credit, and had threatened to cut her off if she didn't curb her spending.

"Cut me off," she'd screeched. "I'm the fucking wife of the fucking mayor, you can't cut me off. I need clothing to look good when I'm out with you, or do you want me to be seen in rags? Is that it? You want to humiliate me by making me wear rags?"

It hadn't been a pleasant conversation, but one they had to have. Allen needed to know, and be put in his place, about her role in his life. The role that had consisted of her being his wife for the last twenty years, tolerating his choice of friends and co-workers who thought they could denigrate and condescend to her, slapping her ass and leering at her tits when they had parties, and turning a blind eye to the whores he saw. She could have thrown his whores at Madam X's back in his face, but that would wait for the right time.

Meantime, she was pleased that she'd managed to keep her dress free from stains. She smoothed it again and walked out the door.

"Where's Allen fuckin' mayor?" Carmelo barged into the restaurant waiting area waving his gun around. "Where's the fuckin' mayor. I want the fuckin' mayor." Screams rang out, and the maître d' dived for cover behind his station.

Allen had been pacing in the hallway and turned around. "I'm the mayor, what's the meaning of this?" He saw the gun in the hand of the advancing man. "Security. Where the fuck is my security?"

"You fuckin' jailed the fuckin' madam. I was gettin' my girls from her, now I have to fuck the fuckin' street whores." Carmelo strode towards him. "Fuck you, you fuckin' cunt."

Sweat poured down Allen's face and back as he put his hands up. "I have no idea what you're talking about, young man. Put the gun down before someone gets hurt."

"Oh, you'll get hurt all right." Carmelo threatened and moved forward, aiming his gun at Allen.

Cecily strutted up behind her husband. "I'm ready. We can go now."

The gun blasted five times, sending bullets into Allen's chest. His blood spattered everywhere, including onto Cecily. Her face, stole, and dress covered from head to toe in her husband's blood. She watched her husband teeter backwards and drop straight down. Watched the man take bullets in the back by her husband's security. Watched as her world fell apart in one split second. And then realised, now that her husband was dead, she could do exactly as she pleased.

She looked down at her dress and stole. They were no longer pristine white.

*****

Carlyle waited for Josephine in the small client room. When she walked in he motioned for her to have a seat.

"I have bad news."

"What is it this time?" She sighed and slid into the chair. "Is Allen refusing to drop the charges?"

"Ah, no. The new mayor might, though."

Stunned, Josephine stared at him. "What? What new mayor? What the fuck happened?"

Carlyle breathed in slowly. "Something bad, Jo. Last night, a guy, they think a gang member, stormed into the restaurant Allen and his wife had been dining in, and gunned him down. He in turn was gunned down by Allen's security who had been outside the restaurant. Allen and the gang member are dead. Allen's wife Cecily is fine, but in shock, as are the other restaurant goers."

Josephine sank back. "What does this... Wow."

"Yeah. I know. It's made the papers and the news this morning. As for what this means for you. I have no idea. I've contacted a few people in power that you know, and found out that they're keeping quiet for now until a new mayor is decided. But it looks like the assistant mayor will step up for now. I spoke to Bernard Dietrich, the politician, he had spoken to Allen a few minutes before about getting it sorted. But, with other politicians on Allen's back about going forth with it, who knows what the hell's going to happen now."

Josephine breathed out. "Fuck. So what do I do now?"

"Wait. There's nothing else *to* do. I do want to go over your financials while I'm here. Now your assets are still frozen, I'm trying to get that undone. I need to be paid, obviously, but so do your bills, and the girls, and your staff. What do we do with everything?"

"My will is with your firm, as you know. Everything is

to be left to one person. But if anything happens to me here in jail, or if I'm sentenced and not released, use the money in my account to pay for everything. If the government doesn't take that first. I've dealt with a few things in the last month, already passing on some of my belongings and putting others into storage. My money has been squirrelled away into accounts in another name. The person with that name can pay the debt if there's nothing left in my accounts. But the house, the furniture, my belongings all go to them. *Do not* sell the house. There are still valuable items in there that I can't get to and I don't want you going in for because I don't know what will happen to them if you do. Take the money, not the house. How much is my bill now, anyway?"

"A couple of hundred grand. But the more this drags out, the more it will cost and it's coming out of my pocket until they unfreeze your assets."

"They have the house, I want the house passed on. You need to get it back, Carlyle. You need to get all of it back. I have a very bad feeling about all of this. Eugene, Everett, Isadora, now Allen. Something's happening. Two forces are working against each other and I'm in limbo and something is *very* wrong."

Carlyle saw the panic on her face. "Don't worry, Jo. It's Thursday, I'll try and get back to court on Monday, but unless another judge takes over, no one's telling me anything, so you'll stay here where it's safe."

"Is it?" she interjected. "Is it really safe? For how long? I'm just lucky I have someone here who can help. And what about you? Is it safe for you? What if something happens to you?" A chill rushed down her spine and she shivered. "See what I mean. Someone just walked over my grave. What if someone's out to get everyone and it's not me? What if two factions are working against each other? Those who want me to go to jail, and those who don't? What am I supposed to do then?"

Carlyle chuckled. "You're sounding like an old spy movie, Jo. Calm down. Nothing's going to happen. I'll check in tomorrow if I can, otherwise, you'll just have to be here until we find out what's happening. Take it easy, Jo. I'll talk to you again." He rose to his feet to leave, but she stopped him.

"And let your staff know not to sell my house." She stood beside him. "If something happens to you and they take over, they need to know not to sell my brownstone. That needs to go to the one person who will avenge all of this."

Carlyle flashed a bemused smile. "There's no need for an avenging angel, Jo. You'll get out."

She fiercely shook her head. "No, Carlyle. I won't. I know it in my bones. Something's going to happen. *Do not* sell the house."

"No, Jo. We won't. I'll make a note of it when I get back to the office. Stay strong." He squeezed her hand and left the room.

"No, Carlyle. I have a feeling you won't." The shiver sped down her spine and she knew it was true.

*****

Sonja Ryan paced her office. As the interior designer to the rich and famous in New York, she had an expensive showroom in the heart of old money. An established corner in the Upper East Side.

But it was now, as she thought about the dastardly plan she'd concocted with Alec, that she wished it didn't have glass walls on two sides. Even though she was on the third floor of the showroom, which held her office and en suite, she wanted privacy. Privacy to think, to plan, to revel in her evil, but also fear the retribution if she pulled it off. There was no one who would come after her. She was sure of that. It would end with her plan and it would all be over. The threats, the fear of being recognised that she lived with every day. The dread in the pit of her stomach.

She twisted the ring on her right middle finger in circles. A habit she had when afraid and nervous. But she had to do something. Something to help her family. To keep her secrets hidden. Because apart from her and Alec, only Josephine Pompadour knew them. And that needed to end now.

*****

Carlyle drove away from the remand centre and headed back into town. He called his assistant to gather the lawyers dealing with the Madam X case to gather in the conference room for a powwow. He needed to update them on Jo's will and papers.

He steered onto Park Avenue to get him to his Upper East Side law firm. A five-storey building he owned outright and was paid for by fifty years' worth of wealthy clients like Josephine Pompadour.

"She also doesn't want the brownstone sold to pay for the debts. We need to get her assets unfrozen ASAP so we can get paid. I'm not far, I'll be there soon."

"You're cutting out, did you say we're to sell the brownstone?"

"No, don't sell the brownstone. Don't sell," he yelled and pulled into the green lit intersection to turn. "*Do not* sell the brownstone—"

The truck careered through the red light straight into his car, sending it across the intersection and into the corner of the building facing him.

Carlyle was dead on impact.

Chapter 12

Bernard met with Cyrus in his office. "So what do we do now?"

Cyrus watched him get comfortable on his sofa and offered a drink. "About what?"

"You know full well about what? Allen, Josephine, this whole bullshitting catastrophe." He accepted the drink and knocked it back. "Allen is dead by some punk's hand, and didn't get Jo out of jail. She's still there. We need her out. To not only stop her from speaking, but to get back to running the brownstone."

Cyrus sat in the easy chair opposite him. "I don't know, Bernard. Do we really want to go back to that? Maybe this is giving us an opportunity to move on with our lives and straighten out."

Bernard regarded him. "Harlan was right. You really are a weak, lily-livered man, aren't you? You had no problem going to her, but once someone put out the signal to arrest her, you melt into a puddle of piss. Weak, Cyrus. *Piss* weak."

Cyrus scowled. "I am not, and don't you dare say otherwise. My thinking is that this has happened for a reason none of us had any involvement in, but someone did if they forced Allen to have her arrested. Now, with Allen murdered in cold blood, in front of his poor Cecily, no less, we have to deal with another mayor and lord knows who that will be or what they will do when it comes to this case. Either we need to let this case come to its natural conclusion, or we need to get her out. Either way, I no longer want to be implicated in this. I'm cutting my ties with that kind of lifestyle and am done with it."

Bernard laughed, a raucous, rough kind of sound. "You have got to be kidding me? You, give up going to a madam? That'll be the day. You're in it as thick as the rest of us, Cyrus. But with Allen gone, we need to get on this and put pressure on someone. Who can get her released with minimal fanfare?"

Cyrus hauled himself up and paced the room. "I have no idea. And I'm not going to ask, because you know full well people will start asking why we want to get her out and possibly add two and two and get four and realise many of us are in on it. No." He swept his hand across in front of him. "I'm done. I am done with brothels and whores and Josephine Pompadour and Madam X."

Bernard rose to his feet. "You're a fool, Cyrus. If she goes down, then I for one will be out for revenge. Watch your back, because it won't be just your wife gunning for your balls. So will I and everyone else." He wrenched open the door and slammed it behind him.

Cyrus walked around his desk and sank into his chair. "Who can I call?" he muttered. "Who *is* there to call? And what the hell happens to us if anything happens to Madam X?"

*****

The men met at their regular gentlemen's club seating section. It was the same one every time.

Harlan puffed his thick Cuban cigar. "Gentlemen. I have a feeling this may be the last time any of us see each other."

"And why's that?" Howard asked, nodding at the waiter who delivered their drinks. He waited for him to walk away. "Why's that?"

"MX."

Howard glanced at him. "Why would that have anything to do with us not meeting?"

Harlan looked at each man. Howard, Donald, Bernard, and Prentiss who had turned up for the first time in weeks. "Prentiss, surprised you're here."

"So am I, but then you did call." Prentiss smiled grimly. "Why did you want me here?"

"Because we were all there that night. We saw the demise of a thriving business. The demise of our one little luxury we could all keep a secret. And I have a bad feeling, with Allen being gone, that this trial will continue and bring all of us to light. We cannot let that happen. We cannot let the next mayor or judge bring our secrets to light, gentlemen. What are we going to do about it?"

"Cyrus wants out," Bernard told them. "The lily-livered pussy. I saw him this morning and he wants out. Believes this is our one chance to change our lives around and get out of it before it's too late, considering what happened to Allen and all."

"He's not wrong," Donald conceded. "It *is* a chance for

us to get as far away from it as possible, in the hope our careers aren't damaged, because many will be."

"I'll be fine, it's the norm for me." Harlan finished his drink and ordered another. "But you politicians, judges, and lawyers, you'll lose big time."

"Thanks for the vote of confidence, Harlan," Howard said dryly. "While I may be a producer, I may not get off scot-free even though many a producer has done very wrong things and gotten away with it, others have gone to jail for their dirty deeds."

"Same for directors," Donald added. "Not too many of us have been caught. But now this…" He shook his head and looked out the floor-to-ceiling windows into the dark night.

Harlan glanced around the room. A handful of powerful elites lounged in wingback chairs sipping their favourite liquor, puffing their illegal cigars, and reading their daily papers. He chuckled. "But I have a feeling, if anything happens, many of us will be. Are you prepared, gentlemen?" His gaze landed on Prentiss. "What about you, Prentiss, being a cop and all. Has the commissioner hauled you in yet?"

Prentiss winced. "He did, after Bartholomew's body was found. He didn't say much of anything, just that I should change my nighttime activities if I wanted to stay on the force, and while he couldn't demote or fire me for what I'd done because he couldn't prove anything and couldn't arrest me, either, it was a warning."

"Is that why you haven't been here for a while? Or at Madam X's?" Harlan asked, blowing out smoke rings.

Prentiss nodded. "Figured I'd better lay low, and then

bloody Allen had her arrested. Does anyone know what's going to happen now he's dead? I've heard nothing."

There were a few murmured nos and then silence which Bernard finally broke. "But what do we do now? And what if something does happens to her?"

*****

The officers entered the building where the Carlyle law firm resided and asked to see the person in charge. They were directed to Mallory Huxley on the fifth floor. When they arrived, they saw a woman approaching them.

"Officers. Mallory Huxley. They rang me from downstairs. You want to speak to me?"

"Ma'am. Officers Heathcote and Barney. Can we talk in private?" the female officer asked. "It's important."

"Of course." Mallory escorted them to her office and closed the door. "So, what's this about? Should Carlyle be here? Although we can't seem to find him. We were meant to have a meeting earlier, but he didn't turn up." She walked around her desk and stood facing them.

"This *is* about Mr Houston," Barney replied. "We've just come from a traffic accident. The victim was Mr Houston. We're sorry, ma'am, Mr Houston is deceased."

Mallory grabbed hold of her desk and sank into her chair. "No…" Her head shook and her eyes glazed over. "No…"

"Ma'am. We found Mr Houston's wallet and business card, saw he was a lawyer and came to see you as soon as possible. We're sorry for your loss. Did Mr Houston have a wife, or children? We need to talk to the next of kin."

"Ah…" Mallory shook herself out of her daze. "Wife is deceased a couple of years ago, never had children. But like all good lawyers, he had a will, so his estate will be passed on." She covered her mouth with both hands. "Oh…"

"And what role do you play, Ms Huxley? Here at the law firm?"

"Ah…I'm his associate and head of the entertainment division."

"Did he have partners, in the firm. I see his name everywhere. Are there no partners?" Heathcote asked.

"Ah…no." Mallory shook her head and crossed her arms, hugging herself in comfort. "He never wanted partners, could afford to hire lawyers and keep the business to himself. I'm not sure what happens now, I know he had documents made for the company."

"Do you know who takes it over?" Heathcote glanced around the office. It was as luxurious as the rest of the building. High-end finishings and furnishings.

"I think I do, but I'm not sure. He did ask me at one point if I would want to stay on if anything happened to him. The company would have to stay in his name, but I would run it via a trust. I said it was up to him who he left it to." She frowned in thought. "I think he set up a trust."

"So, there's no one to contact. No next of kin at all? Siblings, nephews or nieces?"

Mallory looked up out of her reverie. "His siblings are also gone, they were older. He has a couple of nieces and nephews, but wasn't close and I don't think he'd leave them anything. It's all going to depend on his will, and who comes out of the sewer I suppose. From what I know, his estate is large. Several buildings, investments, stocks and bonds, bank accounts, shares. Quite large."

"And who is his lawyer for all of this?"

"Not someone from here, that's for sure, but understandable." Mallory dug into her office diary and pulled out a business card. "Never thought the day would come I'd have to hand this over. He told me to keep a copy because they were his lawyers, and if anything happened, to hand it over." She held out the card. "His lawyer. Another bigwig of New York."

Heathcote took the card and read it. Chesterton Charleston. Charleston & Associates. "Thank you, ma'am, we'll leave you now." With a nod, she and Barney left, closing the door on the now sobbing woman.

They travelled a couple of blocks over to Charleston & Associates and was welcomed into the office of Chesterton Charleston himself.

The rotund man in his three-piece navy suit with the light blue tie and pocket kerchief motioned at the two chairs in front of his desk. "What can I do for you, officers? Please, take a seat."

"No, thank you, sir, but you may need to take one," Heathcote said. "We have some bad news?"

"About?" Chesterton sat behind his desk and picked up his cigar. "Do you mind?"

Heathcote shook her head. "No, but you're a lawyer, you know that's not allowed."

He chuckled. "My office, my rules. What can I do you for?"

"Mr Carlyle Houston passed away in a vehicle accident this morning. We've just come from speaking to Ms Mallory Huxley and she gave us your card as you're his lawyer and are dealing with his estate." Heathcote held up the card. "We're sorry for your loss."

Chesterton stared at them, his cigar forgotten. "He's what? Carlyle… Gone…"

"Yes, sir." Heathcote nodded. "This morning in an accident. Ms Huxley told us you did the work for his estate. We're informing you, so you can start proceedings and contact anyone who needs to be informed."

"Yes…" he said distractedly. "Yes… Thank you. Oh…" He leaned back in his chair and stared out the window. "Damn it. You never know when it's your time and you're going to go. Damn it."

"No, sir. Thank you for seeing us." Heathcote put her hat on and turned as the door opened.

"Chesterton, dear, are you ready for lunch, although it may as well be dinner by now. I know it's late but I… oh, I'm so sorry. I hope I didn't interrupt." The woman in head-to-toe Chanel came to a stop and stared from Chesterton to the police and back.

"No, no. This is my sister, CC Charleston, publisher extraordinaire. We're having lunch. CC, the police officers here just informed me that Carlyle Houston was killed in a vehicle accident this morning."

"Oh, no." CC's hand flew to her mouth. "Oh no. I have many authors who are with Carlyle. Oh, no. This is awful. What happened?"

"A truck ran a red light and smashed into his car, from what we know, he didn't suffer," Heathcote said. "We'll leave you now, thank you, Mr Charleston." She nodded and followed Barney out the door, closing it behind her.

"Fucking hell!" burst out of CC. "He was the lawyer for some of my authors."

"And I'm the lawyer for more. Yes, this is going to be an issue. Especially one case in particular that he was dealing with."

"Josephine Pompadour's?" CC lowered herself into the chair at his desk. "Poor Carlyle. Poor Josephine. What the hell's going to happen now?"

"Now, we go to dinner. Tomorrow, I deal with Carlyle's estate, and you deal with your authors. Next week, we deal with everything else."

*****

The two men jumped the back fence and ran to the back of the house, lifting the kitchen window, and hauling themselves inside. This was potentially the last time they would get to do this, and it had to be done now.

They tore through the cupboards, floorboards and wall cavities. Ran into the library and searched under every floorboard they could get up, and tried pulling the shelves off the wall. They moved into the parlour and did the same.

Nothing. They came up empty handed.

They made their way up to each floor and ripped apart every room. The john's rooms, the maid's rooms, and finally Josephine's room. With them still devoid of furniture there was nothing to check except the floor and the walls. And they'd done that twice already.

One sighed and ran a hand through his hair while the other hand perched on his hip. "This is ridiculous. What are we meant to find that neither of us found the last two times? What if it's in her possessions which have been removed?"

"Don't know, but we were told to come here and check," the other said. "Last stop is the basement."

They hurried downstairs and pulled apart the three bedrooms before going into the laundry and pulling the washing machine away from the wall. They opened it, pulled it apart, but found nothing. They looked in cupboards, but found nothing. They passed the toilet with a cursory glance inside, then backtracked and checked the cistern.

Nothing.

They went into the sex room and found nothing was going to be buried in the concrete walls and floor.

"That's it then." The eldest walked out of the room with fond memories of getting his ass spanked by the madam. It was a sad day that they'd no longer be able to do that since she'd been arrested. By their father no less.

"We may as well go. It's not here which means she still has it."

"Or her lawyer has it which could be a problem. If Carlyle's got it, what then? What happens to all of us then?" Connor stared at his younger brother. "Pop said she had a list. Said she denied it. If it's not here, where the fuck is it?"

Declan shrugged. "No idea. But let's get the fuck outta here before someone hears us and calls the cops."

"You know we *are* cops. We could say we got here first." Connor followed him up the stairs to the landing. "But what are we gonna tell Pop?"

"The truth." Declan stopped at the kitchen door. "That the list is nowhere to be seen and neither of us have found it all these times we've come looking."

Connor nodded and followed his brother out the window, closing it behind him. They rushed over the fence and ran off down the street.

The woman came out of the shadows of the underground walkway, hands in pockets, hoodie over her hair and face. She had heard every last word as she'd used the microphones and cameras Josephine had installed in the brownstone to see what was happening during her incarceration. And she didn't like one bit of the words spoken. Two Ryan men, two officers of the law, breaking and entering and trashing the brownstone all on the orders of Douglas Ryan, ex-NYPD commissioner.

The knowledge burned her through and through and the one thought that went over and over in her head was, *that family is going to pay.*

*****

Josephine walked into the family room at the remand centre on Friday morning. She hadn't been expecting anyone else but Carlyle, although he had said he may not turn up, so was surprised to see Sonja Ryan in her disguise. "Sonja."

"My name's Deirdre," she whispered furiously. "Sit down, we need to talk." Her gaze darted around to see who could be watching.

"About?" Josephine sat opposite her. "What do you want, Sonja?"

Sonja glared daggers at her. "My name is Deidre, call me that. I need to talk about you being in here and what you're going to do about knowing me."

Josephine put her hand up to stop her. "First, your name is Sonja, I'm not playing your bullshit game. Second, what am I going to do about knowing you? Of course I know you, you decorated my brownstone years ago. What the hell are you on about?"

"I meant before that." Sonja glanced over her shoulder and fidgeted with the ring on her right middle finger. "You know full well what I mean."

Josephine regarded the person before her. Former whore who worked for her, turned interior designer extraordinaire, all thanks to meeting Alec Ryan when he came for his night with a girl. Once he had Sonja he hadn't wanted any other, and after a year of using her services, stopped coming. Soon after, Sonja stopped working for her, and the next time she'd seen her, a year or two later, she'd changed her name, died her hair, and had a makeover. She'd also had a son, married Alec, and started an interior design business. "Sonja, your life is yours to do with as you wish. I have no need to reveal it. I've never revealed anyone's business, I really don't know why everyone thinks I will now. Everyone's secrets are safe with me. No one needs to worry."

Sonja leaned towards her. "All well and good for you to say, you're in here. The rest of us are out there and people are dying off. Did you hear about Allen?"

"Gerard? Yes. I did. Carlyle told me yesterday. So sad," Josephine mocked. "And Eugene and Everett before him, Bartie before him. Yes, you are starting to die off, aren't you. Meanwhile, I'm here waiting for one of you to get me the fuck out of here."

Sonja shrank back at the anger. "Sorry, but there's no way in hell I'll be doing that. You'll have to wait for your lawyer. But what happens if you get out? What then? Where will you go? What will you do? Will you start up again?"

"Probably not." Josephine watched Sonja carefully. She fidgeted with the ring, and her gaze darted around. "I'm too old for this shit now. And the brownstone's destroyed. They destroyed your hard work."

"Yes, I did hear," Sonja replied. "Pissed me off, that did. All of my goddamn hard work destroyed by my own goddamn family. I don't think I'll be able to find those wallpapers again. They were rare or one-offs. And the furniture, priceless antiques."

"Most of which I had replicated and switched out, so the originals are safe." Josephine glanced over Sonja's shoulder at Angelo, the guard, her one friend in the place. "But that's of no concern now. Why did you come here, Sonja? Or was it just to threaten me?"

Sonja leaned across the table. "You need to keep your trap shut about me and Alec. No one can know what happened."

"Sonja, enough. I had enough of this last time, and I've had enough of it now. This is tiring. I have no reason to say anything. Now, if that is all?" Josephine stood to leave, but Sonja dashed around the table and grabbed hold of her arm with both hands, pinching the soft skin of the underside. "Say nothing, Josephine. Do you hear me, say nothing."

"Get off me," Josephine yelled, trying to shake her off, but it took two guards to pull Sonja off her, and she watched one guard haul her out of the room.

"You okay, Madam?" Angelo asked, reaching out for her.

Josephine looked at the inside of her right arm. Halfway up the inside of her forearm was a small red dot that was itching like crazy. "I think she pinched me, or something. She left a mark." Her brows furrowed and she remembered the ring Sonja had played with and flashed back twenty years earlier when Sonja had talked about her grandmother's ring that could poison men. Soviet Russia was a harsh place to live. Sonja had turned the ring upside down before jumping at her. "Oh…" The panic set in. "I need to get back to my cell now, and stop that woman, get her ring. I think there was poison in it." Josephine rushed off for her cell and grabbed her notebook and pen. Turning to the last page she scribbled, *Carlyle, Sonja Ryan was just here to see me, she wore a shoulder length brown bob wig, brown contacts, and black framed glasses. She was wearing an ugly brown and beige jumper and a beige corduroy skirt. She called herself Deirdre. She fidgeted with a ring and I think she pinched me with it. I fear it might have been poisoned as I now have an itchy and very angry red blotch on my right inner forearm. If anything happens to me I need you to get this notebook to Sydney Kingston. You have her details, she'll do what's right. They've done it, Carlyle, they've killed me. The bastards have killed me.*

She signed her name and dated the note.

Angelo rushed back in. "We didn't catch her, Madam,

but I was given some news. Your lawyer has been killed in a car accident. It happened yesterday." He watched her grow pale at the news. "Madam?"

"Carlyle," she whispered, her bottom lip quivering. Her one true and loyal friend. "Carlyle's gone?" She took a breath and started again. "That woman was Sonja Ryan." Josephine grabbed an A4 yellow envelope from her stationery kit. One luxury she had been allowed to have this last week. "Wife of Alec Ryan, who is the son of the police commissioner. I think she poisoned me with her ring. I just wrote a note to Carlyle in my notebook…" She paused and caught her breath. "They're coming for us. Carlyle, and now me. We're doomed, Angelo. Can I trust you with an errand?"

"Anything for you, Madam." He moved to her side. "You look deathly ill."

Josephine showed him her arm. The red rash was spreading. "Poison. They've killed me and my lawyer." She quickly wrote on the envelope. "I was going to tell you to get this to my lawyer, but now I don't trust anyone except for one person. Take it to *Pulsate Publishing*, tell them you have a parcel for Sydney Kingston from Josephine Pompadour, and deliver it yourself. Even if CC Charleston is there, you must see Sydney in person. Don't trust anyone else to get it to her. Hand it to her yourself." A sickening wave washed over her. "It's too late for me, nothing can help me now." Her heart raced, then slowed, and her vision blurred slightly. "Pack up my things and make sure you get them to my housekeeper Hilda. Her number is in my address book, along with others. Make sure she gets everything and tell her to pass it on to my heir. She knows who. I feel…" Her head drooped.

"Madam." Angelo helped her onto the bed. "Is there anything I can do? I'll get the doctor."

"It's too late, my dear friend. Just know, that I kept my mouth firmly shut while I was in here, and if anyone dares to say otherwise, remind them I kept their secrets until Sonja Ryan killed me." Her head dropped onto the pillow. "Get that notebook to Pulsate and Sydney. Get my things to Hilda. Tell my lawyers I was poisoned by Sonja Ryan. Promise me."

"I will, Madam." Angelo gently held her hand. "I'll do everything you've asked."

The other guard came to the open door. "What's going on?"

Angelo glanced over his shoulder. "Madam thinks she was poisoned by the visitor who grabbed her. She became very ill very quickly."

The guard rushed in, took one look at her, and saw the rash on her arm. "Damn, I know that rash. It's poison all right. We couldn't stop the woman though." He radioed for the doctor, fearing it was already too late.

Josephine's breathing laboured and she barely managed to mumble, "Make sure my things are given to… My notebook to her…"

"Madam?" Angelo watched her eyes close and felt her neck. The last breath left her and he shook his head, sadness washing over him. "She's gone."

The doctor rushed into the room. "What's going on, poison, did I hear?"

The second guard motioned to Josephine. "The rash on her arm, I've seen it before. It's fast acting and needs one prick. Angelo says it was the visitor she had. Pricked her arm with it."

Angelo stepped aside for the doctor who checked for a pulse, and then checked the rash. "Yes, I've seen this. Moderately fast acting, one has around ten to fifteen minutes to live, if that. Damn!" He gently placed Josephine's hand across her chest. "We'll have to deal with this. Did she say anything?"

"Just to make sure her belongings are given to the right people," Angelo said. It's not like he was going to tell them anything else.

During the time her body was taken by the facility's coroner, Angelo packed up her belongings, took the envelope back to his station, and looked up Pulsate Publishing. He rang for CC Charleston and told her he was calling on behalf of a prisoner at Edgecombe, Josephine Pompadour, and she wanted him to pass along something to Sydney Kingston. Could he arrange a time to come in and see them both as he needed to hand it to Sydney personally.

While completely unusual, out of curiosity, CC agreed, and later that afternoon, after closing time, Angelo was let into the office of Pulsate by two guards and taken to meet the publishing house owner, CC, and Sydney, her new up-and-coming Australian author who was writing thrillers under the pen name Cassandra Kingsley. He told them what happened with Josephine and handed over the envelope.

Sydney removed the notebook and flicked through it, reading the last page. Her blood boiled and her tears overflowed. She held the book against her chest and quietly sobbed for a few seconds before remembering where she was. Nodding, she retrieved a thousand dollars from her purse, offering it to Angelo. "You were with her in her final moments. She wasn't alone, thank you."

He put his hands up in protest. "No, I can't and I won't. On principle. No, thank you. I liked Madam, and she was always nice and kind to me, a motherly figure, if you will. I did this because I wanted to." He pointed to her tear-stained face. "I take it she meant something to you, too. Were you a former girl of hers?"

Sydney choked back her laughter, but managed, "No, no I wasn't. Just someone who knew her for quite some time. And you're right, she was motherly. Thank you so much for bringing this to me. It must have been hard today."

He nodded. "Yes, it was. But I promised her I would do this and here I am. For Madam."

"Thank you," Sydney said. "The guards will show you out." Holding the notebook to her chest, she wandered over to the floor-to-ceiling window and gazed out at the overcast evening. That morning's weather report had said it was going to be sunny, but during late morning, the clouds had come over and stayed. Clearly to grieve for what had transpired.

Sydney thought about Josephine and all of the plans she had. Plans that would no longer be happening. "I'll make them happen for you. I'll avenge you, mark my words. And one day, I *will* have my revenge on the *entire* Ryan family."

Chapter 13

"It's getting harder and harder to renovate this thing." Katie Millgrove swiped the back of her arm across her forehead to get rid of the sweat. "It's been a year and we've barely started. I'm beginning to wish we hadn't bought it." She gazed up through the rafters of the five floor brownstone they had bought a year ago in a desecrated state. Floors and walls had been ripped out, ripped up, and destroyed to the point of removal. What was once a gorgeous and stunning brownstone had been reduced to shambles. "We've had to remove all of the wall panelling, which is a shame because it was original wood and some had amazing old wallpaper on it. And pull up half the floors on every level, and gut it back to its core."

"And then we had all of the trespassers who thought they could get in and rip it up some more," her husband, Malcom replied, throwing down his hammer. "I need a break because this is back-breaking." He pulled a can of cola from their cooler and sculled it down. "How many times have we started something just to find more damage the next day? And we had to wait three months to take possession after the sale. And then we had to organise everything just to get started. Building permits, which were not forth-coming, neighbours had an issue. I just…" He collapsed onto a chair and looked around at the roughed up concrete floor that had been under the damaged wood flooring. "At least we managed to pull down the walls of the bedrooms and make this one big space."

"And reorganising the rest of the space to make a larger laundry and storage area helped." Katie sat beside him and sighed. "I love this place, but Jesus, every time we do something it's been pulled down or ripped up by trespassers. What the hell are they looking for? It's just a basement. They can see that the rest of the house is gone. Nothing to see here, folks."

Malcom gazed around at the open space. "We've put the walls up for the rooms, that big basement room can be used for more storage or whatever. We need to finish pulling out the toilet, to remodel it, but the laundry is done to the point we can waterproof it."

"We should wait until we do the toilet. I have no idea why we left it. Why didn't we pull it out with the laundry?"

"Probably because we were keeping it as is, and the laundry was leaking water and the walls joined with the others. The toilet's in its own little corner over there. I'm surprised they left it alone for the most part."

"Probably didn't think a toilet room needed pulling apart," Katie mocked. "They destroyed everything else, including the bathrooms upstairs."

Malcom peered up through the floors. "Half that floor is still intact, but the others aren't. Bastards. I can't believe they ripped out walls and floors. What a goddamn waste."

"And not one we can afford." Katie replied. "We've nearly run out of money, so unless a miracle happens, or your family can put in work for free…"

"Yeah, yeah." Malcom laughed. His whole family was in the construction business and had readily offered their help in rebuilding. "We did tell them they could. I think my dad's picked out all of the wood, and he and my brothers are ready to come in and relay everything when we're ready."

"That might be sooner than expected. The budget's low. We should go and have a look at that toilet. The water's off, right?"

"It is. May as well, so we can get it all done at the same time." He hauled his weary body to his feet and trundled into the small toilet off the large storeroom. "I wonder if we could make it bigger?"

"It's big enough." Katie stood behind him and crossed her arms, leaning on the door frame. "It has a nice sink and towel rack. And the wallpaper's pretty. I'm surprised they left it alone."

"They did, but trespassers haven't, because some dipshit's broken it, so it needs replacing, and the wall's got a hole in it." Malcom reached down and hefted the broken toilet bowl away from its hole. It ripped away from the cistern plumbing and a splash of water came out. "Definitely needs to be replaced," he muttered and carried it out to the wheelbarrow where he dumped it. "We'll have to add that to the list." Walking back into the toilet room, he dusted off his gloved hands. "How much does a toilet set us back, these days? And are we buying it brand new?"

"Of course we are. We can't put a second-hand toilet in a toilet room for people to use. Gross." Katie stepped aside for him. "Just the cistern and then we can clear this place out. We're keeping the sink. It's intact."

"Surprisingly." Malcom grabbed hold of the cistern and pulled it. A chunk of wall came away with it and a large plastic bag fell to the floor.

Katie jumped back in fright. "What the hell is that?"

"A plastic baggie full of books." Malcom set the cistern down and picked up the bag. "A zip bag full of ledgers and notebooks, by the look of it."

"Oh, my God, do they belong to her?" Katie grabbed at the bag and it popped open. She pulled out a small black leather notebook and flipped back the cover. "The Clients of Madam X," she read from the front page and gasped. "Oh, my God, it is." She flipped through the pages, but couldn't read any of it. "I have no idea what this says. You?" She handed it to him and pulled another book from the bag. It was a ledger in the same coded writing as the little black book.

"Looks like code, maybe. No idea. But if this does belong to Madam X, then we could sell it and make a motza. All our financial issues would be over and we can finish renovating this house."

Katie looked up in surprise. "Who would we even approach for that? And how do we put out that we have Madam X's client list? It's not something we could broadcast to the world. This is probably what people have been after all these years? What they've trashed and vandalised this house for. The client list."

Malcom nodded. "You could be right. This is a goldmine,

but we have to be careful." He slowly turned the notebook over in his hands. "It could be worth a small fortune to the right person."

"Or our lives to the wrong person," Katie replied. "That story was sensationalised. It's why we bought this place. We thought it would be funny to own and renovate Madam X's brownstone. Instead, it's brought us nothing but trouble."

"True." Malcom pondered the idea moment. "We need a broker. Not sure which type. But a broker who can put feelers out privately and quietly to those who might want to buy it."

"But if the buyer is the wrong person, they could come here and murder us to try and get it," Katie suggested. "We need to be super careful."

"We do." He returned the notebook to the bag and zipped it up. "We do."

*****

After consulting with their lawyer, Warwick Buckner, he put a quiet word out to the one lawyer he knew was interested in the brownstone, Chesterton Charleston, who had been hounding him for the last year about getting the buyers to give up the house to its rightful owner, or, at the very least, sell it back for what they'd bought it for.

Warwick informed the Millgroves that Chesterton had someone who was very interested in their items considering that the original law firm dealing with Madam X's will had sold the brownstone against their client's wishes and not passed it onto the rightful heir.

His client *was* the heir and they were intent on doing a deal for ownership of everything so they could finally own what was rightfully theirs.

After Chesterton consulted with his client, and discussed with Katie and Malcolm the unfortunate events that led to the house being sold and not passed on, it was kindly suggested there would be many a nefarious person who would hunt them down for Josephine's books if they went public with them, and this was the safest bet if they wanted to stay alive and still make some money out of it.

His client was willing to pay the price they had bought the brownstone for, and for the renovation of the house to the highest standards, bringing it back to life as the home it used to be, as cost was not an issue. The client would reclaim ownership of the property immediately by having the deed put in their company's name, pay the couple a princely sum for their work each year the renovation went on, and allow them to rent it out for an undisclosed amount of time to recoup money for themselves. But, when the time was right, the client would take ownership and they would move on with whatever money they had earned. The client would not, however, be paying for the books they had found, as they rightly owned those and they would fall under the cost of the brownstone and renovations being paid.

Everything would be silenced under both a confidentially agreement and a non-disclosure agreement for the rest of their natural lives, and whatever the new owner claimed about it moving forward in order to keep their privacy would be considered the truth. The Millgroves would have no recourse under the agreements.

Katie and Malcom read over the contract from Charleston & Associates, had their lawyer go over it with a fine-tooth comb, had the implications of owning the books and what selling them in the real world would mean explained to them again, and how, after the debt they had fallen into would be removed, they would be able to renovate the brownstone without the pressure of paying for it, receive payment for doing the work, and still earn on top of that by renting it out. They talked it over, and as Katie was done with doing it all herself, and owning a cursed home, they agreed, knowing they would get their one million dollars back, plus one million for the start of the renovations and security guards to stop trespassers and thieves. They had doubled their money for something they should never have been allowed to own in the first place.

By the end of the week, Katie and Malcom had a two million dollar check in their hands.

And Sydney Kingston had Madam X's brownstone and client list in hers. She was pissed that she'd had to pay for something that was rightfully hers by law.

Carlyle's assistant had misheard his call that last day, and thought he'd told her to sell the brownstone. His firm illegally sold it for one million when it was worth twelve point two, but the damage done to it by the NYPD meant it wasn't going to sell for that price and the law firm knew it. They needed to dispose of assets as quickly as possible because they were desperate to be paid and hand out wages to Josephine's staff and girls, and to end their association once and for all with Madam X. They couldn't get into the frozen bank accounts, and she'd moved much of her money into her secret accounts, and stocks and bonds, *after* paying her taxes, of course. She wasn't about to get into trouble for tax fraud. The one million barely covered the costs for the law firm.

Not long after, once probate was completed, they handed Josephine's estate, and the rest of the Pompadour assets including those handed down from her mother and grandmother, over to Sydney and her lawyers Charleston & Associates, even though they had sold off part of Sydney's inheritance. They didn't apologise, and Sydney went after them for the money and illegal disposal of assets. Mallory Huxley hated paying out the money, but because they had sold off assets they did not own, they were forced to as the judge declared they were in the wrong, but the brownstone would not be returned to Sydney. Mallory was duly removed from the company by the trust running Carlyle's law firm after his death. The trust included Carlyle's lawyer, Chesterton Charleston, who saw to it his friend's law firm stayed in good repute, and made sure to handpick Mallory's replacement with someone he knew Carlyle trusted.

Sydney flew into New York to complete the deal, hand over the check, sign the contracts, and take ownership of the brownstone. She gave Katie and Malcolm her plans for her new home and asked them to consult with her regularly about the renovations which they agreed to with no issue. All bills would be paid via her company and law firm, Charleston & Associates. She also had ownership of the books, which she wrapped in fake book covers, carefully concealing their real potential, and drove back to L.A. as she didn't want airport staff inspecting her luggage.

She'd recently moved to L.A., after ten quiet years in New York getting to know Josephine. She'd become an author while there, and her three self-published e-books had hit it big, becoming best-sellers. One was being turned into a movie after negotiations for a mega deal, and she thought it best to be in the thick of it in Hollywood.

She made it safely back home after two hotel stays on the way, and had her assistant, Amy, with her, who worked on deciphering the client list while Sydney drove.

"Do you have them?" Emerson Lake, Sydney's new best friend and the writer, director, and producer extraordinaire who was making the movies based on her books, excitedly bounced from one foot to the other in Sydney's luxurious sand-coloured kitchen diner where she had been waiting all morning. "Open the bag, open the bag."

"Calm down." Sydney laughed, and extricated them from the clean zip bag she had put them in. She laid each down on the table and removed the fake covers from them. There they were. Multiple ledgers in different colours, and the one book everyone wanted most of all. The little black book with the client list.

They were all finally hers.

And all fake as hell.

"Goddamn!" Emerson released a long slow breath. "Where do we even start? *Do we* even start? Are they exactly the same as the originals?"

"Not one bit." Sydney picked up the black leather notebook and started flipping through it. "Jo made copies of each book, with fake names and other info. No one knew every book was in shorthand. No one could read them except for her and anyone else who knew it, and she made sure all of it meant nothing if anyone got their filthy paws on it. She knew something was coming, and told me so on the Saturday when she switched the books out and gave them to me for safe keeping. It was in case something happened, which it did. She knew they'd try something, just didn't know what or when, and was disgusted by what they did do, but was glad the fakes were in place. I'm just glad the pigs didn't find them on the Sunday." She took a breath. "Amy, have you written all of this out in plain English so we can see what she wrote?"

"I have. Jo knew her shorthand and so do I. Thanks to you driving on the way back, I managed to get it deciphered and it's bizarre. All gobbledygook that means nothing. I printed it out as we pulled into the garage and collected the original list and books from your safe on the way back from the printer." She handed over the two stacks of A4 paper and bag of ledgers. "It still icks me. The thousand names, their jobs, their physical descriptions, and their fetishes. So disgustingly gross!" She wiped her hands on her jeans. "I did not need to be reminded of that again. How revolting are those men?"

Sydney chuckled and handed the fake notebook to Emerson, before sitting down at the head of the kitchen table and scouring the original papers. "Even now I still can't believe I know so many names on this list. Actors, directors, producers, singers, musos, Harlan Conway. He owns that gross men's magazine, doesn't he."

"*The biggest tits in the nation.* Isn't that his magazine's motto?" Emerson shook her head and closed the notebook, sitting down on the long side of the table. "All Greek to me. What about the ledgers? Are they the same?"

"All shorthand rubbish. I'm still shocked so many famous people are on this list. Parker Grant, and that muso called Romeo. Parker died from a drug overdose about six months ago, and Romeo was involved in a prostitute scandal and left his burgeoning new career."

"Parker Grant the former kid actor?" Amy asked, sitting opposite Emerson. "I used to like him. Damn, that's right, I remember he died. It got out that he'd used a madam. Oh…" Her eyes widened and her lips formed an o. "He was one who had the extreme fetishes and had been a druggie since his teen years. Damn! How many were outed during the case?"

"Only a few during," Sydney replied. "We leaked the photos of Eugene Haskell and Everett Lloyd to the Press, and dug up the dirt on Isadora Crawford and passed it along to those who needed to know. But the others held lots of money, and lots of power. They were all scared Jo would reveal their names while in jail, but she didn't. Her lawyer asked them to recuse themselves from the case, but only Everett Lloyd did. Eugene died of a heart attack, and Isadora was fired by others with more power than her. When Jo died in jail, we stepped up the attacks, and kept ousting more as revenge."

"And now we're here in L.A. to carry on the baton," Emerson crowed. "Can we cross off anymore names? How many died by their own hand? Have any died recently?"

Amy hurried over to the small desk next to the kitchen bench and grabbed a red Sharpie, giving it to Sydney as she sat back down. "Yeah, I want to know how many are gone. Dead or retired."

"Quite a few, if I remember." Emerson bit her lip in thought. "That director and producer both disappeared. Howard Herchel and Donald Reinhold. A few judges did too, and then some were found dead by their own hand, or of natural causes."

"Yeah, *natural* causes." Sydney snorted. "Revenge was done and dusted for them." She went through the one and only original printed list and looked at all of the names that had been crossed out in red. "Amy, hit up Google." By the time they had googled every other name on the list to recheck their status, it was dinner time and two hundred names were marked off as dead. "Wow. I didn't realise we weren't up to date with how many had taken to their demise in the last year and a half, even though we pushed for it with all of those lovely explicit photos we sent to them inferring we'd release them to the public as revenge for Madam X. And some we did release. They chose to go out their own way instead of ruining what career they still thought they had to avoid the scandal. Others left the limelight, but they all had a hand in her demise. And that's what we sought revenge for. How many just retired and disappeared?"

"One hundred and one, but I can't find anything on them, so they could be dead, too." Amy scrolled though a website. "Maybe we should hit up the New York obits to see."

Sydney snapped her fingers and pointed her forefinger at Amy. "Great idea. Can you get started on that and I'll go through the paperwork from her lawyer and figure out our next step."

"I've already thought of that," Emerson said, her excitement escalating. "I have a plan!"

Sydney perked up. "Oh. And what plan would that be?"

"Well, my plan is to find the men who moved here in the last year and a half to get away from the scandal, especially after retiring, and go after them. Surely more of the judges and politicians are old and frail by now. A heart attack must be imminent. And I am gorgeous and could give a man a heart attack just by being me." She flicked her long black curls over her shoulder, and smoothed her hands over her curvaceous figure.

"Heart attacks *will be* imminent once they get a load of you," Sydney agreed. "Especially with those breasts. Are you going to use your feminine wiles on them to procure these heart attacks?"

"Absolutely. Anything to get revenge. This is the most exciting period of my life. Who knew what doing a family tree could find you." Emerson picked up the list and read the names. "I happen to know a few of these men personally, the actors, directors, producers, some of the singers and musicians too, pretty much any who resides here in L.A. in the TV and film industry. Too many have had a crack at me, thinking I wanted them in my pants. Ugh, gross and hell no. But I can start dropping hints, talk about doing a movie on the infamous Madam X, see what reactions I get. I'm even thinking of creating a TV show on real life crimes. Maybe I could suggest that my first series will be about Madam X. I already have a name for the series. *Twisted Minds.*"

"Great title. Think it'll ever come out?" Sydney asked.

Emerson glanced up from the list. "What, their

involvement with Madam X or my TV show?"

"Our relationship to her." Sydney cocked a brow and grinned.

Emerson mused on the comment. "It's always possible. With DNA, and TV shows always doing a who's who of relationships, and this is your life style shows. It could come out that we're third cousins who share great-grandsiblings and have only just found each other these last couple of years." Her smile moved from Sydney to Amy who smiled in return.

Sydney made a sound under her breath and stared out at the California sunset radiating through the sliding glass doors of the kitchen, before glancing at Amy and then Emerson. "Is there such a thing as great-grandsiblings? But really, who knew, that when you did your family tree, you'd find out that your great-grandfather was the older brother of a brothel owner from Russia, who made her way to America and had a daughter who took her place, and who went on to have a daughter to take her place. Or that he and she had a sister who went on to have children, who went on to have Amy here as a granddaughter." Sydney motioned at her assistant who grinned.

"And who knew, that when your father passed away the truth would come out about your real mother being the *current* brothel owner." Emerson giggled. "You should have inherited everything. Including the men."

Sydney chuckled dryly. "Yeah. Except I didn't because the house was sold off to pay for her debt. But, I'm glad dad never knew that I knew before his death. Because I'd done my own family tree over a decade ago and found out I had Russian blood in me. I also found out she'd written me letters and sent cards, but I never got them thanks to mum and dad burning them. That pissed me off. They never told me my real birth mother was in America. Or that Dad had a fling with her while separated from his wife, and she thought I'd be safer with him in another country considering her life choice. He reconciled with his wife and she adopted me as her own. I never knew until it was too late. No wonder our relationship never felt right. She was my stepmum not my mum."

Emerson reached out and squeezed her hand. "She was a good one, though, wasn't she? And your dad a good dad? And at least you were able to communicate with Josephine these last, what, ten years?"

"Yeah, I did, thankfully. And I have her first name for my middle name, and she was the one who named me Sydney. The one thing she made my father promise to stick with. My name. Sydney Josephine Kingston. So I know the whole story of my birth, her life, the scum who trashed her house that day. I was so disgusted by it I ripped her lawyer apart. But then I remembered Jo had told me she'd had replicas made of her heirlooms and furniture and the real pieces were in storage. I'll be having some of the replicas repaired and maybe sell them off for cash, or keep them for extras, or if you guys want something, they're all yours." She shrugged. "All of the real pieces were handed down from great-grandma to grandma to Jo, and she gave most of the jewellery to me while she was alive, and wore the replicas, plus the few personals pieces she kept wearing which came to me while she was in jail as she wasn't allowed to wear jewellery in the remand centre. I collected those items while she was in there and she said I may as well keep them, especially if something happened to her. Which it did. I'll treasure the real pieces."

Sydney glanced at her left hand and saw the rings Josephine had worn from her mother and grandmother. Josephine had never taken them off, until jail, nor the small flower studs that Sydney now wore daily in her third pierced hole. The Cartier watch was left for formal occasions along with the other jewellery she inherited, and the majority of the fabulous Victorian era clothing was in storage while a few pieces in her favourite colours hung in her wardrobe. Josephine's other clothes and accessories were with everything else locked up tight.

She played with the diamond ring on her middle finger and flashed back to when she first met her mother.

Staring up at the brownstone, Sydney took a deep breath and mounted the stairs, trudging one foot in front of the other until she was standing in front of the vestibule door, her shaking hand reaching for the bell.

Why? Why am I shaking? Why am I so nervous when I've been talking to Josephine for months, and writing letters every week. I know her. She knows me.

The door flung open and there stood the woman herself.

Josephine's hands flew to her mouth in shock. "Oh... Sydney...oh..."

Sydney just stared back, her heart in her throat, nerves twisting her gut in knots. "Ha-hi?"

"Oh, my darling, do come in." Josephine pulled her into the vestibule and shut the door, then led her into the

hallway and closed the internal door. She looked at her daughter. "Oh, my darling, I just…" The tears fell. "I never thought this day would come, but I hoped it would." She pulled Sydney into her arms and hugged her fiercely. "Oh, my darling, I finally get to see you, and meet you, and hold you, and love you." She stroked Sydney's long brown hair. "I always wondered what you turned out like. Always knew this life, my life, was not for you. Hell, I was surprised when I found out I was pregnant. The affair with your father was short-lived, but amazing. And being pregnant with you just as much. But I knew this life wasn't for you." She held Sydney at arm's length. "But look at you. From your letters I know you've had an amazing life, a great family, friends, a career. This life isn't for you, but, I guess, you'll get to see it in person now, and get to know me in person." She cupped Sydney's tear covered face. "We finally get a chance to be together and learn to know each other. My darling, Sydney. My darling daughter."

Sydney came back to the present. She'd had a good ten years with her mother, seeing her every day, being shown around her new home, getting to know the woman who had given her life and then given her away. Living in The Big Apple in a small apartment that Josephine owned near the brownstone, having a life that her mother paid for, taking lessons and classes in writing, English, crime, technology, history and so much more, seeing the sights and getting to know everything about her ancestry. The Russian American parts of her, as her grandfather was American. They had a lot of time to make up for, and make it up, they did. Sydney had even used her ancestry in her recent novels.

"Um, here, can you read this and tell me what you think?" Sydney asked Josephine as she handed over a clipped stack of paper. "I used some of your family's background for the inspiration, but I don't want to give away too much detail. It's for my writing class. Well, I started it in my writing class as a short story and before I knew it off she went. It's my first real try as an author."

Josephine took the paper and glanced at it in surprise. "You wrote a novel? Oh, well done, darling. I can read it today. Will you be staying?"

"No, I have classes. Just wanted to know what you thought of it." Sydney shuffled uncomfortably on the spot. "Considering I didn't grow up here, or with you, I'm not sure you'll like it, using your family and all, but you can tell me if I used too much."

"I'm sure I'll love it. You go to class and I'll get to reading it and tell you what I think when you get back. Will you be coming by this afternoon after classes?"

"I can, I know your nights are busy." Sydney raised a jaunty brow and grinned.

"All except Sunday night which we spend together," Josephine reminded her. "You run along and I'll get to this." She ushered Sydney out the door. "I'll see you later, darling, don't be late for classes."

Trepidation followed Sydney all day as she mechanically moved from class to class, dreading what her mother would say about her story. She'd been writing since she was a child in school, and while her stepmother and father had encouraged her, and she'd done some writing for magazines after leaving high *school, she hadn't felt confident enough to tackle a book. But now that she was living in New York and taking writing classes, she had.*

That afternoon, when she arrived at the brownstone and met her mother in the parlour, Josephine looked at her in shock.

"It was awful wasn't it!" Sydney declared and covered her face with both hands. "I knew it. I should never have thought I could write a book just because I got an A on the story for writing class. It's awful."

"Don't be so absurd, darling, it's wonderfully fantastic. You're such an incredible writer. You absolutely need to take up writing full-time. Write more books, become an author, I know people in publishing, you know. My lawyer, Carlyle, his lawyer is Chesterton Charleston. His sister, CC, runs Pulsate Publishing. I can set you up a meeting. Have you written more books. You'll be the hottest new author around, darling. The toast of the literary world."

Sydney's hands lowered, and her jaw slowly dropped. "What? You like it? Why?"

Josephine laughed and sat Sydney down on the royal love seat by the window. "Why wouldn't I? It's well-written, with rounded out characters and plot, it's intriguing with its twists and turns, and that sex scene, woo. Sydney, have you been spying on my girls, because you have that position down pat."

Sydney's eyes widened in horror. "Oh, God no. No, no, no." She rushed to her feet and waved her hands in protest in front of her. "No, no, no, I most certainly have not. It's just my imagination, and something I might have tried with a former boyfriend." She blushed. "So… you liked it? It's not too heavy on the Russian stuff?"

"Liked? I loved it!" Josephine sprang up to stand beside her daughter. "No, it's not too heavy on the Russian stuff. Some of that didn't even happen to me, or my mother, or grandmother, but some of those other things did, so some truth is fine. You're an amazing writer, Sydney, you need to do this as your occupation, because I certainly don't want you partaking in mine. Steer clear of my career as far as you can. And I've been thinking…" Josephine grinned. "I can tell you about the johns that come here, and their careers and fetishes, that might help if you go into crime thrillers. And then there was this one woman who worked for me from Russia, who ended up marrying the police commissioner's eldest son and changed her whole persona to become an interior designer. Woo, is that a story unto itself, so is that entire family. The previous commissioner whose only son is the current commissioner who has four extremely good looking sons. But I can definitely get you a meeting with CC. I've met her a few times, she's quite the character herself."

So was Josephine, and she'd visited her mother in jail twice a day. Once in the morning, and once in the afternoon.

Sydney kept playing with the diamond ring on her finger as she thought back to her last visit that Friday morning.

"You have everything you need, right?" Josephine asked. "I really don't know if I'll be getting out of here, Sydney. I have this feeling in my gut that I won't make it to trial, and so I want you to know how much I love you,

and I'm so glad and grateful that you contacted me all those years ago and wanted to come and see me and spend time here getting to know me. I wish I could hug you one last time." Josephine's hands went to her mouth and her eyes swelled with tears. "I love you, my darling. Please do what you can to those who need it done to. Only you can get revenge if anything happens to me."

"Oh, I will, don't you worry," Sydney told her, tears gushing down her cheeks. "I'll get revenge on all of them no matter how long it takes. I have the time."

"But I don't. Regardless of the trial starting on Monday. I don't want you there. I don't want you to have to see what they do to me."

"I'll be there," Sydney said, and reached out both hands across the table.

With a sneaky glance at Angelo, who nodded, Josephine quickly reached across and squeezed her daughter's hands. "I love you, Sydney, never forget that."

It had been the last time Sydney had seen her mother alive. Because, by the afternoon, Josephine was gone and Sydney was at Pulsate receiving her notebook from Angelo. She swiped away a lone tear.

"And now you have her client list, her ledgers, and *finally* her brownstone, which should have gone to you in the first place." Emerson sighed and felt ready for bed, even though it was early evening. "What are you going to do?"

"Besides still being pissed off at her law firm for selling my bloody brownstone when they weren't supposed to. I should *not* have had to buy that back. But…" Sydney deflated with a sigh. "On top of the books, she left me several properties in and around New York and Long Island, including the apartment I lived in for ten years, and a fair bit in her safety deposit boxes. I have a tonne of stocks and bonds that would bring quite a handsome sum of money if I cashed in, millions left over that didn't go to the lawyers or pay for the house in the bank account she kept in my name, her own family tree findings, and decades of diaries belonging to her, her mother, and grandmother and their papers and books, plus the furniture and keepsakes, her clothes and accessories. I also had monthly updates of videos and photos of her clients, which is why I was able to release them. And before she was arrested, she sent me extremely detailed letters of every man on the list. Their fetishes, their birthmarks, and copies of the evidence of their behaviour. She knew how to email and used it. Thankfully, that Bartie Winthrop garbage is gone, and his wife is being quiet. God help her if she's not, because I'll release that footage. I have everything I need to exact revenge on who's left. And, after everything Jo told me about Mary's very illegitimate son born to her when she was just thirteen, we tracked him down and can release that information as well, just to get back at her. Bet poor diddums has no idea her son was Allen Gerard, New York's mayor, who she harassed into arresting Jo. Thank God Jo slapped her a couple of times. And then he was gunned down by some dickshit john who had used her services, that Caramello Koala wanker of a gang leader."

Amy snorted and burst into laughter. "Wasn't his name Carmelo, not Caramello?"

Sydney's tired laughter joined hers. "Yeah, it was, but

his name reminds me of the chocolate bears when I think of it, even though he looks nothing like a koala. It's an insult to Caramellos *and* koalas." Sydney's laughter grew louder and Emerson soon joined in. They spent several minutes getting their composure back.

Gasping in a few breaths, Emerson finally asked, "And how long do you think this will take?" She noted how worn out her long-lost cousin looked. She felt it herself. "And when do we start?"

Sydney chuckled. "How much energy do you have, and how many of my books do you plan on making into movies? I've written three more and plan on releasing another next month. I did my deal with CC just before all of this happened a year and a half ago, so she's got the paperbacks and hardcovers churning out. As for the men, we can start with those here in L.A., maybe get help with some in New York, and see how many we can get with one stone."

"Maybe we could release some of that footage and imagery. Just let it all hang out there? Send some to that trash rag, *The Enquirer*," Amy suggested. "I'd love to see them all die of shame."

"Maybe, *if* we can do it all quietly and not draw attention to ourselves," Sydney shot back with raised brows. "I don't want people to know we're doing this because I sure as hell don't want to get myself into trouble. We need to keep this plan quiet. We need to keep our bloodline quiet."

Emerson nodded in agreement. "That would be necessary, even though we look nothing alike with Amy being Russian American Asian, me being Russian American Jewish, and you being Russian American Australian."

"True," Sydney said. "Even though we're all Russian descent thanks to our great-grandparents, we're mixed with other things and couldn't possibly be considered related. But we can get back to sending photos and videos to people and see what happens. Gain traction again." Her evil grin lifted the corners of her lips. "I wish I could see the looks on their faces when they hear her name or open their package."

"So do I," Emerson agreed. "But we've got a lotta work to do, so let's start with those we can start with."

"Maybe I should change my name to Pompadour," Sydney suggested. "No one else has it, you know. That would really freak them out."

"Maybe you should write a book on Madam X and secretly add a lot of those still alive in it under different names. *That* would really freak them out." Emerson chuckled.

Sydney made a mental note. With everything she knew, she'd already made numerous handwritten notes, had some scenes in her head for a novel, and had plenty of information for a biography. Plus, she had the real client list. A cast of a thousand, with two hundred already dead by their own hand, another hundred missing in action, and one New York family that was to blame for all of it who would pay dearly sometime in the future. She was going to hunt down the rest until they were all gone and had paid for their sins. She had their names. She knew their faces. She had all the evidence. All the ammunition she would need.

She smiled and reached out her hands to her newfound cousins.

Amy and Emerson reached out theirs, and they joined, a united troika against the evil who had taken Sydney's mother.

Revenge was going to be oh-so deliciously vindictive indeed!

About the Author

L.J. has been writing since 2006, when her first of many novels, ***The Road To Vegas,*** was born. In 2016 she created the ***Porn Star Brothers*** series about three sizzlingly hot Australian born Greek Island raised brothers who became the hottest porn stars in '70s America.

L.J. lives in Australia, loves '80s music, disaster movies, and collecting Jackie Collins books as Jackie is her inspiration and mentor.

L.J. Diva is the adult pen name for author Tiara King. You can find more about Tiara on her website; follow her on social media, or visit her publishing house, Royal Star Publishing.

Socials

tiaraking.com.au/ljdiva

royalstarpublishing.com.au

Sign up for *Tiara's* Newsletter…

Make sure you're always in the know and never miss free exclusives, the latest news, book updates, and so much more with newsletters from…

tiaraking.com.au

Have you read these?

THE PORN STAR BROTHERS SERIES

Porn Star Brothers
Forever
Love Never Dies
Stefan: The New Generation
DeLuca
Spiros & Jenny
And Always

THE ILLICIT THINGS SERIES

Her
Him
Madam X

A NOVEL INVESTIGATION SERIES

Designs in Crime
A Killer Plot
Murder on the Set
A Novel Investigation (omnibus)

Or these?

NOVELS

Burning Desires
Anything for You
Falling for London
The Road to Vegas
Hollywood Dreams
The Billionaire's Dirty Little Secret

SHORT STORIES

The Body
The Perfect Plot
The Star of Your Own Crime Scene